Masquerade

Georgia Le Carre

Cover design: http://paperandsage.com/site/
Editor: http://www.loriheaford.com/
Proofreader: http://nicolarhead.wix.com/editingservices

Masquerade

Published by Georgia Le Carre
Copyright © 2014 by Georgia Le Carre

ISBN: 978-1-910575-00-0

You can discover more information about Georgia
Le Carre and future releases here.
https://www.facebook.com/georgia.lecarre
https://twitter.com/georgiaLeCarre
http://www.goodreads.com/GeorgiaLeCarre

For SueBee
of the 'Bring Me an Alpha' fame!
http://bit.ly/1wToqdP

"Thank you for *everything* you have done for me, seen and unseen."

Author's Note

Hey you,

I am thrilled that you have taken an interest in this book. Thank you. ☺

Masquerade is my hottest, steamiest romance to date, and features sassy, fiery heroine Billie Black and the mysterious, blond, drop-dead gorgeous sex god who not only turns her sexuality upside down but her whole world too.

Hope you love them as much as I do...

xx

Oh, Sinnerman, where you gonna run to?
Sinnerman, where you gonna run to?
Where you gonna run to?
—'Sinnerman' by Nina Simone
https://www.youtube.com/watch?v=Bn5tiuZU4JI

Table of Contents

One 1

Two 13

Three.. 16

Four 29

Five 38

Six 49

Seven 59

Eight 66

Nine 77

Ten...85

Eleven 92

Twelve...98

Thirteen 103

Fourteen 114

Fifteen.. 129

Sixteen 142

Seventeen 148

Eighteen...156

Nineteen 163

Twenty 169

Twenty-one..176

Twenty-two..181

Twenty-three 185

Twenty-four..191

Twenty five 200

One

Billie Black

'**F**ucking kids,' I swear and bury my head under the pillow, but the irritating ringing of the doorbell continues mercilessly. The desire to go out and throttle them is so strong it makes me grit my teeth.

I pull myself out from under my pillow abruptly and frown. Hang on a minute. I no longer live in the poor end of Kilburn, and there are no kids roaming the corridors annoying people on Sundays here. Also, I have no debts left so it can't be debt collectors either. Not that those lazy fuckers will work on Sundays.

I get out of bed and, walking barefoot to the front door, curiously put my eye to the spy hole.

Whoa!

I draw back hastily, and press my hand to my belly. What is out there is far worse than any debt collector. By far worse. The bell rings again and holds. The sound is jarring loud and...insistent. It's not going to go away. I turn my head and look at myself in the mirror on the wall. My hair is a spiky rat's nest. I pull my fingers viciously through the unruly mess, but it does not improve. The bell goes again. Oh, fuck it! Whatever. I don't care, anyway. I take a deep breath, rearrange my face into one of tight exasperation and fling open the door.

Cor... Look at that, though. Tight black T-shirt packed hard with muscles, he fills the corridor like the Incredible Hulk, only he is all blond, and he makes little kitty clench tight even on a Sunday. Damn this man to hell. How can anyone look that good at this time of the morning?

He removes his finger coolly off my doorbell and smiles a severely attractive smile, before letting his gaze, all wicked and sexy, start roving down my body. It's like having melted chocolate poured all over me. I want to lick myself. *Keep it together now.*

'What do you want?' I demand aggressively.

'To fuck you senseless.'

I don't succeed in stifling the gasp that rises into my mouth. The cheek of the man is astounding. Last night he brazenly introduces me to his girlfriend, and this morning he stands on my doorstep wanting a legover! I feel a fine rage in my veins.

'Fuck off, you cheating skunk,' would, as Ali down the sweet shop would say, be giving him too much face. 'Piss off, I don't want you to fuck me senseless,' would be a lie. So: I nod, and move quickly to slam the door in his lazily smiling, smug face. With lightning speed he lays his palm firmly against the wood and resolutely pushes his way in. I am engulfed by the smell of his freshly showered body. Probably washing off her smell, I think sourly. I don't do the undignified thing and attempt to fight against such a male show of strength. I decide to decimate him with pithy wit instead.

Inside, he looks as out of place as a rhino in a China shop.

'The polite thing to do would be to offer me some tea,' he says, one blond eyebrow arching.

I cross my arms over my chest. 'I'm actually not feeling very polite at the moment.'

He flashes a pearly white grin: wolfish in the extreme. The guy is a walking sex bomb. 'That's just grand,' he says. 'We can be impolite together.'

Pithy wit deserts me. 'Don't make me punch you in the face.'

'You were the best lay I ever had.'

My eyes widen. The surge of pleasure I experience irritates me. I pretend to laugh dryly. 'Is that supposed to be some sort of compliment?'

'Yeah, and a goddamn fine one too.'

Before we go any further, let me first tell you that this man is good in bed. No, make that really, really, really good. Like out of this world good. He butterflied my legs and went to work on my girly bits with the precise dedication of a Swiss watchmaker until I nearly fainted with pleasure. And believe me, I'm the expert in muff diving, since I have been for most of my life a lesbian.

'Well, you were the worst lay I ever had,' I lie.

Unoffended, he laughs merrily. 'Time to make amends, then.'

'Don't you fucking dare come near me,' I warn. I realize instantly that there is not enough threat and too much desperation in my voice.

His moss green eyes glint, dark and dirty. They make me horribly uneasy. I'm not in charge here. We stare at each other and the rush of sexual heat that sweeps over my body makes me feel oddly dizzy. The memory of his touch still burns in my bones. Unable to speak I stare foolishly at him.

The truth is I'm pissed off with this guy for not calling after he promised to, for making me sleep with my phone for nearly a month, for confusing the hell out of my sexuality, and for having a girlfriend who is the exact opposite of me, but as the seconds pass, I am not sure anymore if I am more pissed off with him or with myself for being so pathetic.

The problem is that my pulse is racing and I can't think past the aching throb between my legs. I take slow breaths as my body, the hyperaware Judas, remembers and replays the sensation of all the hard planes, the raw silk of his skin, and the absolute perfection of that one night we shared.

I blink. Big mistake.

He advances, his lips twitching with amusement.

 4

I step backwards, purely instinctive, and he takes another step, and so do I, but in the opposite direction. A warm flush spreads over my skin. All kinds of thoughts are running through my brain. Uppermost: of course he's going to get what he came for. I can already feel his hand on my hips, and the lure of a seriously explosive orgasm. He got me the last time through the same fearlessness of consequences he is exhibiting now. No fear of rejection. Such naked confidence can be mind-numbingly seductive.

He turned my no into a maybe and my maybe into a yes.

And afterwards, when the curiosity and desire had been aroused inside me, he delivered big. I mean BIG. I told myself that I had gone with him because I loved that he did not have a prejudged idea of beauty. He found the spider tattoos on my neck and shoulder beautiful! But the truth was/is, he intrigues me like no other. My body is already craving it. It's only sex, Billie, I tell myself.

I stop retreating when I feel the hard edge of the table against my buttocks. He takes his next step silently. With his hands around my neck he tilts my face upwards and swoops down on my mouth. Sweet mother, Mary. So bad, and so hot. My will is slipping away. What will? It's been a long time. A long time. Bloody hell. He tastes so fuckin' good I want to eat him. I get lost in the raving desire that comes in waves from his mouth into mine.

For a few more pulse-ripping seconds his lips bruise mine, a clash of teeth and lips and tongues. It is brutal, arousing, and totally feral. And then I tear my mouth off. The insides of my mouth are still stinging. He is strong, I'll give him that. Very fucking strong. And that arrogant tilt to his chin. Like he should be in a vampire movie. Like he's never heard the word no.

'I thought you thought I was cute?' he mocks.

'If you like psychos.'

He grins and lifts me up by the waist as if I am a doll and deposits me on the table. My legs dangle off the edge. With both his hands he rips open my nightshirt. The tearing sound is deliciously erotic. Nobody has done this to me before. Underneath I am butt naked. His eyes drop to my breasts. With a slow smile he cups them in his hands.

'I wasn't wrong last night: you've had them done,' he growls and pushes his tongue into my mouth. The man's an animal and I love it.

His tongue drives in as I suck it enthusiastically. So different from a woman's tongue. So demanding. So muscular. Suddenly his mouth leaves mine, and a complaining mewl escapes me. Watching me like a hawk he bends down to take a nipple in his mouth and sucks at it cruelly. I close my eyes and moan. His hands move lower. He spreads his fingers into the thatch of light brown curls.

'A hairy girl is hard to come by these days,' he murmurs. 'You're one in a million, Billie.'

'Fuck you.'

He runs his fingers along the slit. I am embarrassingly soaking wet for him. One finger dips inside.

'Yes,' I gasp. Even that one word sounds incoherent. I want more.

He plunders my mouth. Slowly the finger inside me becomes two and then three. The stretch is delicious, but I want more. I need more. And holy fucking shit, I know where there is smoking more. I reach for his belt.

'Look at you, throbbing for release,' he whispers huskily, and pulling away from me splays my legs open. He watches me, his heavy-lidded eyes roaming my thrown back throat, my excited nipples, my legs spread so wide he has a full view of my pussy dripping and swollen for him.

He tears open the condom foil and then unbuttons the top button of his bulging jeans. The zip comes down and he takes out his cock. This is the thing about us lesbians. We're used to big toys, but this boy's toy—it struts right out at a right angle to his body. In its own way it is an aggressive angry thing with large veins. I'm not really sure if I consider it attractive. Certainly it is not pretty the way a pussy is, but there is something wild about it. Something animalistic and caveman-like.

I watch while he sheathes it and obligingly open my legs wider when he plunges the

raincoated thing straight into me. That scream. It came from my mouth! His large strong hands are underneath my bum tilting me upwards. Whoa...call the police—this is an attack! He fucks me like a wild man. A furious wild man.

We are a violent, hot tangle. I writhe and claw at him, and he rams into me until I come, quick and hard. The world shatters beautifully and becomes more perfect than before. Almost immediately he does too with a growl and expletives. I bet his girlfriend doesn't see this.

I grasp the firm globes of his buttocks. We are both panting hard. Now that I am sated I am back to my rather inelegant situation. We have sinned.

'And you thought you were a lesbian,' he says with such an irritating smile that I slap him, so hard his head jerks back.

'That's the first time...' he mutters.

I raise a disbelieving eyebrow.

'I've been slapped by a woman while I'm still inside her.'

I use both my hands to push him away from me, but I might as well have been pushing at a brick wall. The hands cupping my buttocks are like steel manacles.

'You've had your fun. Now get out of my home,' I force between clenched teeth.

'I'm still horny.'

I tingle at the promise his words hold. I glare at him. 'We all have our afflictions and addictions.'

8

Suddenly I have the fierce and surprising urge to mark him. To let his woman know that he has been with me. I want to claim him. He sucks my tongue into his mouth. Too urgent to be gentle. Then his mouth moves, warm and wet against the side of my neck. I know what he's doing. He's sucking on my tattoos, on the blue spiders. He takes his mouth away and looks at them.

'How did you find me?' I ask.

'Not easily,' he confesses. 'I had to shell out a thousand quid. Must be nice not paying your own bills.'

I ignore the jibe. I'm not about to explain anything to him. 'What happened to last night's posh and world-weary murmur?'

He grins.

'When I first met you, you had a BBC accent. Last night it was decidedly posh and today a trace of Australian has slithered in. Will the real Jaron Rose please stand up?'

'This is the real Jaron Rose.'

'Are you going to fucking get your dick out of me?'

'I will but first let me tell you what you're going to be doing tomorrow. At sharp three thirty p.m. you will bend over this table, your elbows and hands and cheek pressed against the glass, your ass in the air barely covered by lace and some transparent material that rips easily. Baby doll nighties and thongs are my favorite at the moment. What you are doing is waiting for me to come and fuck you like the little bitch you are.'

My mouth drops open.

'The rims of the thong will become soaked very quickly and you will consider using your sweating hands to masturbate to relieve the ache, but you *will* not. Instead you will keep that position, nipples and cunt tingling, and wait. The high heels you'll be wearing—I like black— will make your calves cramp, but you will ignore it.'

My pussy clenches like a boxer's fists, but I pretend to snort.

He ignores it. 'At four I will turn up. You will not turn around to look at me or speak to me. No matter how wide your legs are I will have to correct the position by kicking apart your legs and flipping the last bit of covering over your back, so your ass is totally exposed to me. I will roughly rub your panties, find the jellied part, and dig my fingers into it. You will immediately raise your hips higher to try to catch more of my flesh, and moan the way you would if you were begging for it.

'I'll tell you to be quiet. That you are not to make a sound until I allow it. I will flick your clit through the material and your body will start bucking and squirming. At that moment I will swat you on the fleshiest part of your buttocks just once, but hard. My fingers might strike your clit. It will make your head spin and you are bound to cry out from the surprise. But if you do I will spank you again.

Just to hear you cry out and see the blush spread. And again, until you are panting and dripping onto my hand. Excitement, shame, joy, desire.

'Then I will back off, make myself a cup of tea and drink it while I stare at your reddened ass, ripe for the picking. Once I have had my tea I will undress. Slowly. You will strain to hear buttons, material scraping my skin, shoes sliding away, socks pulling, zip tearing. I will grasp the reddened, burning skin in my palms and feel its weight in my bare hands.'

I try not to show it but his dick is slowly growing inside me and I am starting to want him to fuck me all over again.

'Then I will pull the warm red cheeks apart and holding them apart with one hand I will slide my finger into you, first one, then two and eventually three—the way you like it, the way I did the first night we met. You will moan, and shiver and maybe even grunt like an animal. Your head will start to lift off the table—you are about to come. That is the moment I'll stop and will ask you to touch yourself. You will take your hand off the table and press it between your legs, turning your head to look at me while starting to masturbate.

'"Do you want my cock in your pussy?" I will ask. "Yes," you will whisper. I will ask you again. "Yes, yes," you will plead.

'And that is when I will ram so hard into you, you will shudder and scream and arch and quiver and come in a screaming rush.'

'I won't be in at three thirty p.m. or four p.m. tomorrow,' I say coldly.

'Don't be absurd. Of course you will.'

'If I am bent over the table, who will let you in through the front door?'

'That's my affair. You just assume your position.'

He pulls out of me. And fully erect he takes a step away from me. I close my legs and slip off the table. Expertly, he removes the condom. I watch him pull his underpants up and over the rigid flesh.

'It won't break, will it?'

He laughs and pulls his jeans over the bulge. 'Concern from you is always nice.'

'Don't mistake curiosity for concern.'

He zips up. 'See you at four.'

I don't say anything, simply stare at him.

Two

When the door closes behind him my breath comes out in a rush. Holy Moly! That was unbelievable and that was not enough. I am still throbbing with need. What is it about this guy? I simply can't seem to get enough of him. I go to the fridge and pour myself a shot of vodka. I lift it up to my lips, and put it back on the counter. I don't want to take the edge off the way I feel right now. I light a cigarette and walk onto the balcony. I blow out a smoke ring and my mobile goes.

I pick it up from the coffee table and it is my best friend, Lana.

'Hey,' I say.

'Guess where I am?' she squeals.

Well, it's Sunday. Tomorrow is a working day. Her billionaire banker husband's yacht is moored in the South of France. So the South of France would be my guess. 'No idea,' I tell her.

'The South of France.'

'Brilliant.'

'I tried to call you earlier to see if you wanted to come, but I guess you were asleep.'

'I was. So what is the little sprog up to?' I ask referring to my godson.

'He seems determined to swim across the English Channel.'

'That's my boy.'

'What are you up to?'

I kill my cigarette on the balcony railing. 'Enjoying a post-coital cigarette.'

'What?'

'Jaron came around and we had sex.'

'Really?'

'Unless I dreamed it.'

'Oh my God!'

'That's what I thought.'

'Well, go on then, tell me what happened?'

'It was hot and dirty, and he wants to come around tomorrow for more, but I'm not sure how I feel about it all.'

'Why?'

'I think it's that crazy-eyed girlfriend of his. Mind you, I don't feel bad about him cheating on her. I just hate the idea of him inside her.'

'My, my, I've never seen you jealous before.'

'I'm not jealous.'

'Could have fooled me.'

'Well, he's not available. So that's the end of that story,' I say firmly.

'I don't know what the story is between them, but I got the impression last night that he doesn't care about her one bit. There wasn't enough heat between them to keep an egg warm. It was obvious she wanted to claim him as hers, but he only had eyes for you.'

'Well...'

The doorbell goes again.

'Hang on a minute. Someone's at the door,' I say, and walk towards it. I look through the spy hole.

'Talk of the devil,' I say.

'What?'

'Call you back.'

I look again out of the spy hole. The girlfriend is dressed to the nines in a white pantsuit, a long cream coat, sunglasses and a fringe sharp enough to skin a goat. I turn to the mirror and look at myself. My hair is a mess, my nightie is torn in half, and I have that slack, just-fucked look. With a grin I open the door.

Three

Ebony's coldly disdainful eyes flick down my body and freeze at my torn clothes. We stare at each other. Tangibly above all other emotions, disbelief glitters in her eyes. Her chin starts to tremble uncontrollably and a small, pained sound escapes her glossy lips. Her hands, the two-inch long acrylic nails painted powder pink, rush upwards to cover her gaping mouth.

The smug grin dies quickly on my lips.

I pull at the torn ends of my nightie and hold them together. Suddenly I feel like a total bitch. A nasty piece of work.

She stares at me for a moment longer with hurt, accusing eyes, and then turns away, and runs down the corridor. At the end of it I watch her open the stairwell door and disappear through it to avoid waiting for the lift. I close my door and lean against it.

'Shit, shit, shit.'

Maybe she really loves the guy. I shouldn't have done that. That was just plain cruel, and I'm not a cruel person. Damn Jaron. I go to the vodka and take a huge swallow straight from the bottle. The alcohol burns the back of my throat and splashes into my empty stomach. I shake a cigarette out of the box, light it and go back out onto the balcony. I drag deeply from it. Smoke fills my lungs and grips it. I hold the breath. My body starts mellowing out. I look down and see Ebony running down the street. I exhale slowly. A frown on my face.

'Fuck.'

I didn't go looking for him. She's not my responsibility. He's the love rat, not me, I try to rationalize, but guilt is a grim business. Sleeping with another woman's man has left a sour taste in my mouth. It is the same feeling as accidentally killing the fox that suddenly dashes out in front of your car. Fucking hell, you think, why did you have to die under my wheel? Why didn't you just go and die peacefully in some field?

I flick ash into a pot.

Somewhere in my little brain I had a plan to drop some money into Ann Summers' till. But that plan is wearing a slit throat and shoes with dried blood on them: I won't be wearing no baby doll outfit and waiting stretched out on my dining table for Ebony's man tomorrow. In a way it is a relief. There is something about Jaron Rose that terrifies me. He plays with my head. He sets up cravings inside me that I can't control.

I finish my cigarette and grind it out on the metal railing. I am firm in my decision. I'm *never* going to bed with Jaron Fucking Rose again. I go into my home, close the balcony door, and though I can still smell him, I go straight to my worktable.

I sit down and sketch a little girl's outfit. A white pantsuit with blood red lace frills. It has a round red pocket on it. I hold it away from me. Nice one, Billie. I lean my head back and Jaron pops into my mind. With ruthless precision I push him out and open to a fresh page on my drawing pad.

I will forget him, if it's the last thing I do.

3.30 p.m. one day later.

I glance at my watch. All day I have been a bundle of nerves. I've gone through so many cigarettes I feel light-headed. I go into my bedroom and dress in blue: baggy top and shapeless trousers. The least sexy thing a woman can wear, but then I cannot resist spraying a little perfume.

'Who are you trying to kid?' my reflection taunts.

'I can look good while I'm telling him to fuck off,' I tell my reflection, and sweep on a layer of mascara. My stomach is clenched tight with anticipation. I need a stiff drink. I help myself to an impressively large shot. That helps loosen the knot. I twist my wrist and look at the time.

3.40 p.m.

Right. I smoke another cigarette and pace the floor. Time creeps along.

3.55 p.m. I look at my reflection in the dining room mirror. My cheeks are flushed and my eyes glitter

3.56 p.m. For fuck's sake.

3.59 p.m. I take a deep breath and leaving the living room walk toward the hallway.

4.00 p.m.

Jaron Rose walks through my door, and finds me leaning nonchalantly against the hallway table. He is dressed all in black again. And damn if it doesn't make him look devilishly good. He stops when he sees me. We stare at each other. My thoughts swirl like crazy, untangle and drop into a confused heap at the bottom of my mind. Desire flashes like fire between us. The memory of the hot iron thrust of his cock flashes into my empty mind.

He smiles, a hint of something rich and secret. He should come with a warning. Beware. Undercurrents here. Dark and dangerous undercurrents. 'It's not too late to get on the dining table,' he says seductively.

Even I have to admit: he is über, über cool.

'Most people knock and wait to be allowed in,' I say sarcastically.

'I'm not most people,' he says, and gives me a look so filthy it makes my toes curl.

'What did you do? Steal my key and make an impression of it?'

He grins. 'Nope. I'm just good with locks and clocks. Thought I'd save you the trouble of opening the door.'

'Well, don't.'

'Are you always this unfriendly when someone is trying to be helpful?'

I fix him with an unfriendly, slightly suspicious stare. 'Ebony dropped in yesterday.'

His eyebrows rise, but he doesn't appear in the least bit concerned.

'Right after you left... And when she realized that you had just fucked me she burst into tears and ran away.'

For a moment he stares at me expressionlessly and then he breaks into a grin. 'You opened the door in your torn nightie, didn't you?'

I fidget uncomfortably. 'I may have done. But so what if I did? You're the cheat.'

'Awww... Did she make you feel bad?'

'As a matter of fact, yes, you brute.'

He throws his head back and laughs callously.

I glare at him. 'I'm glad you think breaking your girlfriend's heart is funny because she looked a mess yesterday.'

He takes a step toward me and I instinctively take a step back.

He stops. 'Are you scared of me, Billie Black?'

'No, I AM not.' I put my hands on my hips and glower at him.

'Don't run when I come towards you then,' he says, and walks unhurriedly to me.

My pulse starts racing and for some ridiculous reason my throat snaps shut. Watch out, the warning flashes in my mind, and I have to quell the desire to step sideways—backwards is out of the question since there is a wall behind me. So I stand my ground and hardly flinch when his hand slams into the wall, and he leans one massive shoulder against it, effectively trapping me.

I squirm and look up into those dark green eyes. Oh man! Hurriedly, I drop my gaze to his mouth. Fuck me. I drop it lower to his throat. I am on safer ground watching his Adam's apple bob slightly as he chuckles. The warm flutter of his breath on my forehead is a bit more distracting.

He puts one thick finger on my lower lip. 'What's the matter, baby?'

'You're crowding me. Can you move, please?'

'I don't think so.'

I look up then. His eyes are twinkling with laughter. 'You think this is funny?'

He grasps my shoulder and a finger grazes my throat like a trail of fire. 'Not really.'

I train my eyes on his hair. It is so blond it is like spun gold. I want to twine my fingers through it and pull his head down to my mouth. The thought irritates me. I am not sleeping with him ever again.

'What if I tell you, you've been played?' he purrs.

I jerk my neck away from his touch and look at him suspiciously. 'By who? You?'

'You rubbed Ebony's face in it, and she punished you by pretending we are more than we are.'

I frown. 'Are you trying to say she doesn't care you're fucking me, only that I rubbed her face in it?'

'Sounds about right.'

'That sounds like the most unbelievable rubbish, the kind of thing a man would make up to excuse his bad behavior.'

He shrugs. 'I told you the truth. Believe whatever you want.'

I suddenly remember the movie, *Bridget Jones's Diary*. The misunderstanding was entirely caused because the woman the heroine thought was the hero's girlfriend was actually just a lesbian friend staying over. Once that was cleared up it all ended very nicely.

'Is Ebony a lesbian?'

He looks at me strangely. 'No. Why?'

'Oh.' That's that theory laid to rest. 'If what you say is true why did she turn up at my door in the first place?'

'You'll never know now, will you? Since you rubbed her up the wrong way.'

'You're both mad.'

'I've been thinking about you today.'

'I'm not finished talking about Ebony,' I say pointedly.

'I am. I don't want to talk about her. I'm here because you want me and I want you.'

'Has anyone ever told you, you're pushy?'

'No, everyone else thinks I'm charming.'

'Like James Bond? Smooth charm and brutal purpose?'

He smiles suavely. 'See, we can agree when we try.' He puts his hands around me and pulls me close. Our thighs touch.

My belly starts melting like hot chocolate, but with great determination I put a hand to his chest and lean away. Underneath my palm his heartbeat is steady and quick. The man is impossible to resist. 'I don't like James Bond,' I whisper.

'Are you always so cocky, Miss Black?'

'Truthful,' I correct. I look up at him defiantly. His eyes are hungry.

'I don't like the look on your face.'

'Too bad.'

'We'll have to do something about changing it.'

'So now you're going to force yourself on me?'

'Force you?' He laughs. 'You're gagging for it,' he taunts softly, and leans in, crushing me against the wall. His cock strains big, and hard, and hot, actually impressively hot, against my stomach. The thought of *that* inside me makes my knees go weak. I know he's about to kiss me, and reason and the rest of the world are about to disappear into a hot haze. My whole existence will be just about him and what he is doing to my body.

I watch with a mixture of horror and fascination as his mouth comes down on mine. The kiss is ferocious. Vicious. Perhaps too vicious. I feel blood on my tongue. But it is exactly what I need. I have spent all day furious with him and myself and this raw, unrelenting kiss was just the perfect antidote to my restless, angry excitement. The heady flavor of his mouth and the scent of him make me spiral off. I suck his tongue hard and wild excitement pumps through me. It is so huge and potent it blocks everything else out.

When he raises his face, I am panting like some lust-crazed sex beast.

'That's better,' he whispers, 'because you have been tantalizing me for many, many months.' He inserts a thumb into my mouth and pulls my lower lip down. 'And making me hard at all hours of the night.'

The tips of my breasts ache and I rub them restlessly against his hard abs. The sensation that then brings makes me want to grab him by his fucking golden locks and yank his mouth down to my nipples so he can suck them.

Clenching his big fist in my hair he tugs my face up at him. His eyes scorch my skin. My mouth parts automatically. Surrender is what he is looking for and surrender is what he is getting in spades. With a triumphant smile he takes his thumb out of my mouth, and barely giving me time to breathe let alone think, swoops down.

If the other kiss had been vicious this one is barely controlled. His tongue pushes in while his cock imitates the movement against my belly. My sex clenches hard. God! I so want to be broken apart by this man it fucking hurts.

He cups my ass and lifts me off the ground and slams me into the wall. I curl my legs tightly around him and cross my ankles.

His hand slips into my top and sliding around my waist moves up my back. It makes short work of my bra clasp and moving to the front cups a breast, roughly, possessively. He squeezes my nipple. A fierce frisson of sexual heat hits me between my legs. In an instant his mouth leaves mine and my top is yanked over my head, and my bra lands on the floor. Very briefly my brain tries to grasp at some coherence and tries, actually tries to question the sanity of what I am doing and the answer is obvious. *My life has become a scene from a cheap porn movie*!

But then his lips claim mine again and my brain shuts down. I fucking need this... The rest of the sentence should have been... like a hole in the head. But like I said before my brain has shut down. My blue pants are unzipped while I obligingly unclasp my ankles and straighten my legs to help them slide down my legs, and then my knickers are brutally ripped off me. There I am naked and he is fully dressed. Great. He leaves my mouth and looks down on me. I am dripping wet and shameless.

'Beg me to take you.'

I shake my head. Nope. No way am I uttering words of surrender.

'Beg me to take you,' he repeats. His voice is low and dangerous.

'Go fuck yourself,' I spit stubbornly.

'All right then. Beg me not to take you.'

'You're killing the moment,' I warn ominously.

'Basically you don't want to beg either way.'

'Basically.'

He nods, and bending his head sucks a nipple. My chest thrusts toward his mouth and my brain stops functioning again. He lifts his head and looks at me with a rueful smile. 'Maybe not today, but you'll beg before I'm through with you.'

To my utter frustration and shock he turns around and begins walking toward the door.

'See you tomorrow at seven,' he calls out.

Without his warmth I feel oddly bereft. I had let myself become totally swept up in the moment and now it is shattered. He is the unfaithful lover and I am his bit on the side. This has got to be on my terms too. He can't just come and go as he pleases.

'If you walk out of that door now, don't bother coming back,' I say quietly.

He turns around to face me, lets his eyes travel with leisurely unconcern over my naked body. 'I'll come when I want and I'll take what I want when I want. And there is not a damn thing you can do about it!'

And to prove his point he walks toward me and yanks me to his body so I fall against its hard length. He puts a hand on my buttocks and presses me against his erection. And I have to fight the desire to beg him to enter me.

Looking into my eyes he slowly inserts a finger into my wet folds. I bite my lower lip helplessly. He takes his finger out and puts it into his mouth and sucks it.

'You will be mine,' he says with such presumptuous arrogance that I am struck dumb with disbelief. I stare at his dirty blond eyebrows. Very rakish. Very sexy. My mind becomes a bewildering mixture of fury, sexual excitement, and admiration for his freakishly attractive eyebrows.

He lets go of me, and spinning around walks away from my frustrated body.

I watch his rear end go. The man has a world-class ass, hard and perfectly rounded. And if memory serves, smooth as a baby's butt. He stops by the sideboard, reaches into his trouser pocket and brings out his wallet. From one of its sleeves he fishes out a small piece of paper. He slides it on the sideboard and walks toward the door. At the door he turns and looks at me again, his eyes darkening. 'I'll see you tomorrow at seven.'

Then he shuts the door behind him.

For some moments I don't move. Never in my life have I been so totally and so exclusively involved with and aware of someone. To the point where nothing else matters. Everything about him affects me, the soft blond hair, the deeply green eyes, that silky smile. Even things I thought I would despise in a lover, the hardness of his body,

the arrogance, the domineering streak, excite
me to the point of madness.

Naked, I walk toward the sideboard and
pick up the paper. I unfold it and... It is my
phone number...in my own handwriting.
Whoa! Hold the horses. He kept it from that
first night. All this time. And yet he did not
phone. Why? I take it to my nose and smell the
leather of his wallet. And he did not fear
Ebony finding it either. How strange. How
inexplicable.

Four

A man who carries a cat by the tail learns
something he can learn in no other way.
                                    —Mark Twain

I pull on my clothes and remember that night more than six months ago when I did something I had never done before. I went to a rave club alone. It was a hot and sweaty dive. I had dropped a couple of Es and lost count of the vodka shots I had downed. Some guys had picked me up and put me on one of those giant speaker boxes and I was feeling on top of the world.

It was a crazy feeling, the music pounding underneath me, skin tingling, head buzzing. All around me rainbows of colors flashed and illuminated a sea of dancing, sweating bodies. I felt deeply in love with them and at peace with the whole world. At that moment it didn't matter that my best friend, Lana, had found the love of her life and had less time for me. I even forgot that I had broken up with my long-term girlfriend and that I had arrived lonely and more than a little sad. High as a kite I sat on my throbbing throne, eyes closed, and head furiously nodding to the music: oh yeah! All was well in my world.

Then: someone or something touched my neck.

I opened my eyes and there he was. This blond giant. For a second I thought I was hallucinating. I have seen trains arriving through tunnels and sausages falling from the ceiling while I have been less high. I reached out and touched the giant. My hand hit flesh— well, I call it flesh, but it was more of a wall. So I knew I wasn't hallucinating. I peered into his face. It's really hard to see something properly when you're so off your cake. The lines blur. Sometimes you get the eye color wrong. People's voices sound like they've sucked on a helium balloon. And it's hard to really distinguish features. Everyone's a friendly blob.

He leaned in and shouted near my ear that the spider tattoos on my neck were some of the most beautiful things he had ever seen. I gulped. The music was so damn loud I must have misheard that. Nobody—and I mean nobody—had ever told me how lovely my tattoos were. Was he trying to be friendly or was he trying to pick me up?

I stared hard at him.

In fact, the giant was really good-looking. He had straight blond hair and he was big, real big. His shoulders and chest were massive and packed with muscles. He should have repelled me. I like soft curves—Megan Fox is my cup of tea—but he didn't. I watched the curve of his mouth and experienced that first stirring of sexual curiosity for a man. For a man? Never before. He suddenly wrapped his large hands around my waist, lifted me off the speaker and put me on the ground.

'I said,' he repeated, 'I love your tattoos.'

Ha ha. A really good-looking guy was trying to pick me up. More intriguing, he seemed to be as sober as a judge.

'Are you for real?' I slurred, squinting all the way up at him. It felt as though he must have been at least seven feet tall. OK, that was an exaggeration, but that night, lighted by the searching strobe lights, he seemed absolutely enormous. Huge. His shadow swallowed me whole.

'Yeah,' he grinned.

'You have really gorgeous teeth. Are you American?'

He widened his smile in acknowledgement of my compliment. 'No, I'm not American.'

Then I was too high to notice that he was using his East End working class accent. 'They are diligent about teeth over there,' I said, merrily unaware of the disguise he had affected.

'I want to take you home.'

My eyes boggled. 'Oops!'

'Is that a yes?'

'Oops is always a no.'

'It doesn't look like no from where I am standing.'

He really would make a handsome toy for some straight girl. He was almost edible... To a straight girl, that is. 'You're built for bed and everything, but I'm a dyke, mate, and generally we're not like gay men. We won't befriend straight men. In fact, for the most part we tend to be downright hostile to you lot,' I informed him, smiling benevolently.

'That's only because you haven't been to bed with me yet,' he stated.

Even though I was so fucking high, I was impressed. That kind of haughty, patronizing confidence is near impossible to carry off successfully. And he managed not to sound like a dick while saying something that old hat.

'I like pussy. Pussy I can dominate and eat. But a dick? What the hell does one do with one of those things?' I asked.

'I'll show you,' he purred and ran his fingers along the inside of my bare arm.

I blame the drugs. They made me horny. They made me want things I had never planned on wanting. Before I knew it words I had never dreamed I would utter were pouring out of my mouth.

'I'll fuck you, but I'm not sucking your dick or doing anything else gross like that.'

Another flash of teeth. Hawt! There's no way those are not made in America. 'No, problem,' he replied instantly. 'I'm not too keen on that practice either. Like you, I like pussy.'

When I think back now I'm sure he would have got nowhere without all the other incidentals like I was lonely. I was high. I was drunk. But that night I found him intriguing. I felt the desire for him spread inside me, like a living thing, until it was no longer the music that was throbbing in my veins but the foreign need to feel this man inside me. The thought of being eaten and filled by him was unbelievably exciting. I felt myself become wet. I looked at him hard. Well, as hard as one can under the glow of the tablet.

So we went back to Mr. Luscious's flat. An unremarkable, strangely cold and empty place. As soon as we got through the door he jumped on me. He was hungry! Oh boy was he hungry for pussy. And after he had made me come he picked me up like a doll and laid me on top of his body. His flesh was warm and sweat-slicked. I thought I would hate it. A man's sweat.

But I *loved* it.

As a matter of fact I adored the way I slipped and slid on his big body. Suddenly I was small and delicate...and defenseless. I didn't even hear the sound of foil tearing. And then the big moment. He lifted me clean off his body and impaled me on his shaft. Shit! A cock inside me. Never thought I'd see the day. So totally different from a dildo or a vibrator or a condom-covered cucumber. A cock is thick and hard and warm and...alive. I bounced on it until he erupted inside me. After that he made me rub myself on the bone of his groin until I came.

He stood up and picked me up as though I was a child. I wrapped my legs around his hips and he took me to his bedroom. Another strangely empty place, but I didn't spend too much time admiring the décor or the lack of it: the guy was an insatiable animal. I hate to admit it, but he was better than my rabbit. And that's long-life battery operated!

It was an unforgettable night.

For the first time in my life I was no longer in control. Every time I tried to take it back, he used his superior strength and sexual expertise to subdue me. He was very strict and masterful, so fucking strong that I found myself submitting to his sheer size and force. Once I tried to leave and he simply held down my arms and legs until I didn't have the strength to struggle anymore. Until him I had never had anyone so...well...authoritative in bed before. It was something new, something I was not used to...but something I discovered I totally loved.

In my most secret fantasy—I was a submissive.

Dawn was in the sky and I was hot and sore in a way I had never been in my life. My body really could not take much more and I knew it was time to enter the real world again and take back control of Billie. The Es were beginning to wear off anyway, and I was starting to see him without the chemical glow of 'love'. It would be a good time to get dressed and hop it out of there with an 'Um, sorry, gotta go' farewell.

'I stink of sex. I need a shower,' I said, but apparently it was not time for a shower.

The blond beast pinned me down and had his wicked way with me again. There was something about him. Yes, he was beautiful, but I had seen other beautiful men who left me cold. I couldn't put my finger on it and I can't even now, but that something pulls me to him as if I was an iron filing to a massive U-shaped magnet.

I was still gasping for breath when he raised his head and smiled—slow, wolfish, his green eyes crinkling up.

'Come on. Bathroom,' he said, and sprinted out of bed, pulling me along. At the bathroom door he followed me in. 'Um... I really need to wee first,' I said holding onto the door. He looked at me coolly and said, 'No.'

'What?'

'Don't close the door.'

'I need to wee.'

'So... Fucking wee then.' His eyes devoured me.

So I did with him watching. It was kind of horrible and kind of hot. Afterwards, he picked me up bodily and put me on the edge of the bathtub.

'What the fuck?' I protested.

He opened my legs wide and the more I swore at him the more he spread them.

'Keep them wide open. You're going to love this...'

The look in his eyes! I surrendered.

'Look at your nipples. Look how swollen they are.'

I looked and I swear I had never seen them so raw and swollen. He disengaged the showerhead from its bracket and pinned it with his hip against the bathtub six, maybe seven inches away from my sore kitty and turned on the spray.

It was incredible. Lesbians around the world, take note: the showerhead is a woefully under-utilized sex aid. It massaged all of my sex nicely, but one tiny little spray of water fell without respite on my clit. Faster than any tongue or vibrator. Splash. Splash, splash. Hit, hit, hit. Mmmmm...

Pinned by his watchful eyes I hung on the edge of the bath.

'I don't like being watched when I come,' I said through gritted teeth.

'Tough.'

I turned my head to one side and tried to damp down the reaction, but it was impossible. Dark pleasures cannot be denied. My body moved ahead without me. I closed my eyes.

The hand that had circled my ankle, then insidiously massaged my calf and aroused me, tightened painfully. 'Open your fucking eyes and look at what I am doing to you.'

'No, no,' I moaned.

'Be silent and obey.'

I opened my eyes and looked down at his hands as they stroked the insides of my thighs. His fingers pulled apart my sex lips and the exposed, terribly swollen, well-used bud was suddenly and utterly defenseless against the relentless spray. My thighs began to shake with the approaching orgasm. And then all hell broke loose.

He brought me breakfast in bed, ugh, sausages and eggs. We had to stop eating to fuck. When I was leaving he asked me for my number. I gave it to him. He told me he was going away but he would call me in a month's time.

He never did. And I never got to have that shower either. He sent me home in a taxi stinking to the high heavens of him, of us, of dirty sex.

Five

I can tell you straight off the bat that the next day is hell. I am like a mosquito using the edge of a razor blade as a landing to taxi off. I try to work, but I can't concentrate since my sex is swollen and throbbing and the rubbing of my hardened nipples against the material of my T-shirt drives me crazy. At six o'clock I dress in a V neck blouse and a skirt—and no knickers. First he is going to explain about my phone number and then I'm going to let him fuck me.

By seven I am a living wreck, but what he sees when he walks in is me sitting on the sofa as cool as a melting ice cube. I quirk an eyebrow and cross my legs. The message is clear. I'm in charge tonight. We play by my rules.

'Have a seat,' I tell him.

He stalks over, drags my startled body upright and snaking his palms down to my ass slams my pelvis into him. His erect cock presses into my stomach. I don't know how I had expected our meeting to go, but my body sings with relief. My eyes gaze longingly at his lips, my arms cry to hook themselves around his neck and my body yearns to rub itself like a cat against his hard length. Only my pride keeps my raving nymphomaniac instinct at bay.

I avert my face.

He sniffs audibly. 'Pretend all you want, but I can smell your arousal.' He traces the V of my top down to my cleavage. The desire to press my breast into that broad palm is shocking.

'Stop it,' I hiss.

With a wicked smile he cups my breasts with his hands. They are heavy and tight. He squeezes. I can't help it, I whimper.

'Don't you know crossing and uncrossing your legs is considered an invitation?' he mocks.

'Don't you know lesbians play by different rules?'

'Stop me if you don't like it,' he murmurs.

I bring my hand up and catch his in a firm grip.

'Do you want to know what I think?'

'No,' I whisper weakly.

'I think, my little lesbian, that you've picked up a little addiction for cock. For *my* cock. Nothing's ever been good enough since then, has it?'

I gasp at the arrogance of the man. 'You're a patronizing son of a bitch, you know?' I accuse hotly. 'You said you'd call and then you didn't. Why didn't you call me?'

'It's complicated,' he replies pleasantly, and bringing my hand to his lips starts delicately kissing the knuckles.

It is very distracting, but I am determined. 'Is complicated code for you changed your mind and didn't bother to tell me and then you saw me again by accident at the Van Woolf art exhibition and thought, I'm bored, I'll have another go?'

He stops kissing my hand. His eyes focus on mine. 'Look into my eyes and tell me you really believe that. I thought about you every fucking day. I always knew one day I'd come back for you.'

'One day?'

'I told you it's complicated.'

'Define complicated.'

'Composed of elaborately interconnected parts, complex, difficult to analyze, understand and problematic to explain, et cetera.'

The answer is cheeky and evasive, but the gentle finger under my chin from such a brutally masculine man has the surprising effect of making my throat clog with emotion.

'What's found and lost will be found again,' he says so softly I almost don't catch it.

It is obvious that he is hiding something and that there is a problem somewhere, but maybe I wasn't just a one-night stand. Maybe he *does* care some. And I am not just some anonymous fuck.

'I want to see your naked breasts.'

'Screw you,' I say, but my voice is thick.

'You always played the part of the man, the one in charge, didn't you? You were in control, wearing the strap-on dildo and fucking the shit out of them. Well, there's going to be some changes around here. Guess who's gonna be fucked into submission and like it?'

'You don't know me. You don't know what I want.'

'Don't kid yourself, Billie. What you want is exactly what all women want.'

'And what's that then, Mr. Rose?' I ask sarcastically.

'A dominant man with a filthy fucking mouth who will wet your little panties for you, crucify you with his huge cock, and fucking force you to come again and again, until you can barely walk.' A slow smile lights up his face. 'Guess what, babe? Tonight's your lucky night.'

I didn't want to admit it but I couldn't stop fantasizing about his dick. And even the thought of being dominated by him and being made to submit to him makes my pulses race. It isn't natural to me, but he is right, I want him to completely possess me. To get on top of me and do whatever he desires. I want to be utterly, utterly dominated by him.

I lick my lower lips and with a snarl he throws me on the sofa. Tears my top and bra off me and looks with satisfaction at my breasts. He stands and begins to take his belt off.

'Take your skirt off,' he barks.

I obey instantly.

I hear a sharp intake of breath from him when he sees that I am naked underneath. He drops his trousers and his boxers, never taking his eyes off my displayed body. And I am staring wide-eyed at a very large and angry-looking dick. He sheathes himself in rubber, then reaches out and tugs at my nipples. Small sharp tugs that make my back arch.

He tugs much harder. 'Were you?'

'Was I what?' I grunt.

He grabs my knees and spreads my legs open. 'Were you always the man?' he growls, and pushes his thick meat into me with punishing force.

My head rears back against the cushion. 'Yes, fuck you. I was the man.'

'That's all over with,' he snarls and pulling out of me, slams back in. 'You take what I give you.'

I clench my teeth. My thighs are shivering with need.

He grabs a fistful of my hair and pulls my head farther back so my body is curved like a bow. 'You do not have any say in or authority over what happens when we are fucking, do you understand?'

'Yes.'

'Now beg me.'

'Please fuck me.'

'That's not begging. That's telling.'

'Please, please, Jaron, fuck me.'

'That's just asking politely. Beg, Billie. Beg.'

Fuck him. 'Jaron, if you don't fucking fuck me now I am going to go crazy and hurt someone, probably you.'

He laughs, a deep growling sound, and fucks me with such brutal hunger that the sofa rocks like crazy and I feel myself being jerked about like a rag doll. The sensation is one of total loss of control. Total submission. Total possession. There is no equality. Not even the pretence of such a thing. No woman wearing a strap-on can fuck this hard. He is the man and I am the woman. It even works if he is the bastard using my body for his pleasure. I clench my muscles tight around him and hang on for a mega release. When it comes it is bigger than mega: it fucking explodes inside me. Shuddering into my muscles and shooting into my veins like a shaken champagne bottle.

'Scream for me, bitch,' he orders.

And I do. I howl my lungs out. And as I do I feel him reach his climax. He strains against me and pushes hard into me. For a while we are both silent and still. I hear the sound of the cat next door mewing on the balcony.

He pulls out of me, takes off the rubber, and turns back toward me. He drops to his knees in front of me and spreads my legs open. He strokes his hand upwards and opens my pussy wide and pulls back to look at it. I feel a bit embarrassed because it is still fluttering and clenching and dripping with the aftershocks of my tsunami of an orgasm.

'I've missed this little cunt,' he says.

I stare at him.

'So plump and juicy.'

He plunges his tongue into it and the walls of my pussy clench involuntarily. My hands scrape through his silky hair as I pull him in and grind myself against his mouth. My hips begin to make frenzied jerking movements. I know what my body wants. That thing that only he seems to know how to do—when he traps my clit in the hot wet cave of his mouth and does not stop sucking until I find my release.

I find it in minutes.

Afterwards he sits on the couch and pulls me onto him so I am half lying on top of him.

'Want to go out on a date with me?' he asks softly.

'And be provincial like everyone else?'

He shrugs. 'What's the alternative?'

I think about it. Ever since he walked into my life nothing has been the same. I am doing all the things I thought I would despise and lovin' it.

'What about Ebony?'

'What about her?'

I pause. 'So you two have, like, an open relationship?'

'Something like that.'

'And she's not jealous?'

He bends his head forward to look at me. 'She's not your responsibility, Billie. She's mine.'

Whoa! That last sentence hurt! Like a punch in the gut. My first instinct is to spring away from his body. As if he feels it, he holds me tight against his body. 'Ask me whether I love her.'

I swallow hard and feel glad that he cannot see my face. 'Do you love her?'

'No,' he says very emphatically.

'OK.'

'OK what?'

'OK, I'll go out with you.'

He brightens endearingly. 'Where would you like to go? The opera? To the theater?'

'Why on earth would you imagine I'd want to go and see a bunch of people wailing in a language I don't understand?'

He chuckles. 'We can go to an English production if you prefer.'

'Are you serious? Opera in English kills cats.'

I can't see him but I know he is smiling. 'That's what I love about you, Billie. You say it like it is. So refreshing.'

'It's just a matter of taste. Lana likes the opera.'

'Lana Barrington?'

I nod.

'I met her at the art exhibition, didn't I?'

'Yes.'

'She's a good friend of yours?'

'My best friend,' I correct.

How strange, but his body tenses. 'Hmmm...'

I twist around to look at him, but his face gives nothing away. 'We grew up together. I guess we are more like sisters.'

His body relaxes again. 'She's the reason you have this flat?'

'Yup. I used to live on a council estate and her husband didn't want her wandering around one whenever she came to visit me. So he bought this for me. For a billionaire he's a cool guy.'

He raises an eyebrow. 'How did she meet him?'

I'm not about to tell him the story of how Blake paid to acquire Lana. 'It's a long story and you'll be bored.'

'No I won't.'

I look at him curiously. 'Why are you so interested in Lana?'

'I'm interested in everything about you,' he says, and for some reason that I refuse to investigate further, his claim rings hollow. He runs his hand along my body and palms my breast. I turn around to lie with my forearms on his chest.

'So what am I to you then?' I ask.

'What do you want to be?'

I shrug lightly. 'I can't be your girlfriend, because you already have one. So what else is left? I can be your fuck buddy or I can be your mistress.'

His voice is very soft. 'Do you want to be my girlfriend?'

'Not really,' I say immediately and a shade too brightly. 'I think I'd kinda like to be your mistress. You'll have to take me to insanely expensive restaurants and buy me diamonds.'

His eyes flash. 'Do you like diamonds? Somehow I never thought of you as a diamond girl.'

'I was kidding. I've never owned a diamond. Lana gave me an obscenely large sapphire pendant for my birthday. But it's so valuable I've had to put it in her safe.'

'A sapphire to go with your eyes.'

'That's what Lana said,' I say with a smile and, because he is looking at me strangely, I start babbling. 'Lana says diamonds are actually not precious at all. That diamonds are as plentiful as amethysts and should be priced the same. They are only expensive because their supply is so tightly controlled.' I snap my mouth shut. I've never been a babbling brook before.

'Clever Lana. She's absolutely right. It is a strange paradox of this world that all the things that are truly rare are artificially kept at low prices and the things that are not are inflated to insane prices. The only diamonds that are rare are the colored diamonds and the larger sizes. All the others have no more worth than semi-precious stones.'

Taking my forearms he lifts me up and suddenly I am on my back lying where his legs had been.

'Wow! You're fast,' I say laughing.

'You ain't seen nothing yet, baby,' he says, and never a truer word was spoken.

Six

'**D**ress sexy,' he tells me on the phone.

So I wear the white hot pants that I bought in Thailand, black boots and a red top. When I open the door he whistles, his eyes roving my body. 'You totally nailed sexy,' he says.

'Is he dead yet?'

He chuckles. 'Nearly. He will be by tonight.'

I giggle. 'Good, I like stiff things.'

He takes my hand and puts it on his crotch. He is already as hard as a board.

'He'll do,' I approve.

'He'd better.'

He touches my hair. 'What color is this?'

'Teal.'

'Teal,' he says softly. 'You're the only girl I know who could carry off teal.' His eyes crinkle at the corners. 'You're very, very unique, Billie.'

I warm up nicely with the compliment. 'You're pretty unique yourself.'

He laughs. 'Did it hurt?'

'What?'

'To throw in that little compliment?'

'Not at all. I'm a very good liar.' I grin at him.

He grins back. There is something soft in his eyes. It is the way a parent might look at their child. Indulgently. With pride. It confuses me.

'Shall we go?' I say, shrugging into a light coat.

He takes me to a fabulously extravagant subterranean cabaret club in Aldwych, called Voltaire. A set of neon lights points downwards. We go down gleaming aqua steps illuminated by thread lighting embedded in every step.

'Voltaire,' he says, 'used to be a public toilet.'

'Great. You're taking me to a public toilet for our first date. Very unconventional.'

An enormous bouncer shakes Jaron's hand and opens a bright blue door.

Public toilet it may have once been, but it is now lavish, decadent, and a lot risqué. There is not a bright light, shiny surface, tourist, or cashmere sweater in sight. Instead there are gorgeous fallen angels (waitresses and bar staff with wings) buzzing about serving sophisticated, quirky people.

It made for an edgy, unusual atmosphere.

'Well done. It is actually the perfect location for an illicit affair,' I say with a smile.

He smiles back, a heart-melting smile. 'It always reminds me of scenes from Berlin movie stills of underground clubs from the thirties.'

'I love it,' I say and squeeze his hand.

'I've booked a table but let's have a drink at the bar first.'

Jaron orders a champagne cocktail and I get myself a fluid called *The Control Word Is Voltaire*. It is unquestionably potent and it makes me buzz almost immediately. I twist on my kiss me/lick me bar stool and, facing Jaron, cross my legs. His eyes drop to my thighs.

'So,' I say, and pause until he brings his eyes back to mine. 'What's Ebony up to tonight?'

'No idea,' he says with a carelessly shrug.

'Don't you...um...care about her at all?'

He gazes at me, and suddenly our surroundings drop away, and it feels as if his eyes, which look violet in the red lights of the bar, are boring into me with uncanny perceptiveness. As if he is seeing right into my soul. It does not last long, but they are an incredibly and startlingly disconcerting few seconds. However, his voice when he speaks is amused and light. 'What makes you say that?'

My whole body trembles, but I keep it cool. 'I was just curious about your...odd relationship.'

'Odd?'

I look at the smoothly tanned skin at the opening of his shirt collar. 'If I were her I would be jealous.'

'Are you jealous?'

'Obviously not. I'm not your girlfriend and we're just having fun.'

'Hmmm.'

I take another large sip of my drink. 'This is delicious, by the way.'

A spotlight comes on and falls upon a black drag queen with a truly impressive amount of make-up, a glittery evening dress, and long, trailing earrings that go past her shoulders. Oozing cool, she glides from the sliding door that she has come out from and goes to a small platform that serves as a stage.

She introduces herself as Nina Simone.

Sitting at a piano she tells us her first song will be: *I Put a Spell on You*.

Simone turns out to be eye-bleedingly good. Her voice is so strong and clear it makes the hair on my arms stand up. Her Nina Simone is exquisite. When the song is over she stops, wisecracks, and then smoothly eases herself into the song that electrifies the entire room and defines it as hers. Sinnerman!

> So I ran to the devil, he was waitin'.
> I ran to the devil, he was waitin'.
> Ran to the devil, he was waitin'.

She gets everyone going. I turn at the end of her performance to look at Jaron and he is staring at me. His eyes are intense and almost quizzical, as if there is something about me he cannot understand.

'What?' I ask.

But he doesn't tell me what is truly on his mind. 'Wait till you see the toilets,' he says lightly instead.

'Why?'

'The doors are transparent until you lock them and then they mist up.'

'Sexy! Shall we try one together?'

'Nope.'

'Have you gone conventional on me then?' I tease.

'A: I like this joint and I want to be able to come back and B: I have other plans for you.'

'Oh yeah?'

'Yeah.'

It is an amazing night. I eat chicken—well, I hope it is—I drink loads of Voltaires and thoroughly enjoy Jaron's company. He is charming and suave and attentive. By the time we leave Jaron is stone cold sober and while I am not exactly drunk, I am what you could call merry and what most people would class as very, very horny. The taxi turns into Upper Belgrave Street and Jaron runs his hand along the inside of my thigh. I shift my legs farther apart when his fingers start brushing the crotch of my shorts.

He looks into my eyes. 'Wet?'

'Dripping,' I reply.

The taxi comes to a stop outside a very grand and imposing white stuccoed building. I hop out of the taxi and while Jaron is paying the driver I look around me curiously. The street is completely deserted. I wonder why he has brought me here. I look all the way up at him. I actually love that I have to look up at him. It makes me feel like a child again.

Everything is taken care of. All I have to do is just have fun.

'Come on,' he says, taking my hand and pulling me up the steps to the house. He puts a key in the door, opens it and walks in. I don't generally like exaggerating, but it is fuck balls amazing. I stand and stare, completely speechless!

Gray-veined marble floors, polished to a high shine, pull all the way to what I imagine must be the kitchen. The walls are adorned with large paintings framed in heavy gilt. The ceilings are lofty and there are tall doors, all closed, leading away from the hallway. Then there are the marble stairs with their beautiful, beautiful banister that curves around. I lift my head and see the glass roof at the very top of the third floor.

'Wow!'

I turn back to look at him. He is leaning against the door watching me. His eyes are utterly unreadable. I feel as if I could fall, am falling into those depths. 'Whose house is this?' I mouth silently.

'Mine.'

This multi-million pound mansion belongs to him! My brain does cartwheels. 'Who the hell are you?' I mouth.

His eyes. His eyes. They are impossible to read. 'No one. It's all a game, Billie. Just a game. I'm no one. I just want you. Be mine tonight.'

'And the apartment you took me to the first night?'

He shrugs. 'Mine too.'

'That's where you shag strangers?'

'Something like that.'

'And this place?'

'This is where I shag people I like.'

I lick my lips.

He takes a little device from his pocket and presses it. The lights go down and music fills the place. The sound of the music is seductive. A man starts singing.

I was dreaming of the past. And my heart was beating fast. I began to lose control...

I bite my lip. 'What's the name of this song?'

'*Jealous Guy.*'

I frown. 'And the artiste?'

'Bryan Ferry.'

'I've never heard of him.'

'That's because it's before your time.'

'Jaron?'

'Don't, Billie.'

'Tell me the truth. Why didn't you call me?'

He bends his head. 'What does it matter? We're just having...fun.'

'We're just ships passing in the night. So no taboos, right?'

His eyes change, something flickers in them momentarily. His mood perfectly matches the music. 'Because I knew this would happen.'

I don't have time to think or process his words, because he starts walking toward me.

His eyes are unrecognizable. God! this guy really, really wants me. I swear no one has ever looked at me or wanted me like this. The realization is heady. The blood pumps in my ears. I feel almost deaf.

I didn't mean to hurt you. I'm sorry that I made you cry. I didn't mean to hurt you... I was trying to catch your eyes.

I shrug out of my coat and let it slip down to the floor. Deliberately, I kick it away. I slip my fingers into my top and slowly, slowly pull it over my head. My big and beautiful fake boobs pop into view. I chuck the top away.

I was feeling insecure. You might not love anymore. I was shivering inside. I'm just a jealous guy.

In my white hot pants and black boots I pose seductively for a moment.

And then I do a little shimmy, which makes my breasts swing and jiggle flamboyantly. I get down on the floor and slowly unzipping my black boot slip it off. Then: the other. I lie back down, unzip my shorts and wriggle out of them, sexy as an eel on fire. Underneath, obviously, I am wearing no knickers. I sit up and in time to the music put my boots back on.

I was shivering inside.

I lie back down on the cold marble and rising to my elbows and keeping my knees straight scissor my legs. I probably look really silly with my sex all swollen and red, but I don't care. I just like the way he is staring at me. As if there is only him and me and this stupendous hallway and the rest of the world has fallen off a cliff.

I look up at him through my eyelashes, putting as much sauce as I can into it. 'What are you waiting for, big boy?'

He discards his beautifully cut single-breasted jacket as he walks toward me. His eyes hot, hungry, a stranger's eyes. They never leave me.

He reaches me and stands over me as he unbuttons the cuffs of his shirt and pulls his shirt tails out of his trousers. His eyes are already eating me. Shrugging out of it he flings it to the ground. It falls on top of my coat. He uses the tip of one shoe on the heel of the other to unloosen it. The socks follow. Finally his eyes leave mine and latch onto my exposed sex. I widen the V of my legs. He unbuckles his belt and unzips his pants. He steps out of them and kicks them out of the way. Another song I don't recognize comes on. I guess it's old too. A man sings, *Girl, you'll be a woman soon.*

I make a small sound when his briefs drop to the ground.

'Oh my, Mr. Rose,' I tease in a put-on posh accent. 'I've never quite seen you from this angle, and I have to say it's terribly provoking.'

'Not half as much as the view from this angle,' he says, not even a ghost of a smile on his lips. Dropping to his knees he grabs my thighs and buries his mouth between my legs. I grip the big hard muscles of his shoulders helplessly as a cry rises in my throat and dies there. Ridiculous how good he is at eating pussy.

Seven

The sensation is exquisite. On the horizon a climax glimmers.

'Don't stop... Please don't stop,' I cry.

My teeth start clenching, my head glides on the floor, then I am gone like a spinning top. I come back to the marble floor in waves.

'I really, really like having you inside me.'

He raises his head and looks searchingly at me. Then he puts a hand out and gently brushes away a damp lock of hair. 'And I really, really like being inside you,' he says and inside me his cock twitches.

I giggle and wriggle and wrap my hands around his neck and pull him down. 'Are we going to spend the whole night on the marble floor? I think it's really beautiful but I kinda like pillows, duvets and mattresses.'

'So do I, baby,' he says, and with a single graceful movement bounds up and, pulling me up, puts his shoulder to my stomach and hauls me up and over his shoulder. He carries me nude, but for my shiny black boots.

'You are such a caveman,' I scold, shaking my ass suggestively.

'Just claiming what is mine,' he says cheerfully, and with a firm slap on my naked bottom, carries on up the stairs while I giggle like a crazy coot. I've never been carried up a staircase. It is a heavenly feeling. One I would have scoffed at and never thought I would enjoy.

Another singer I don't recognize is crooning, *Is this love?* Jaron doesn't look old but... His music.

'How old are you?' I ask his back while I watch the movement his pert ass makes as he climbs the stairs.

'I'm a thousand years old, Billie.'

His mood has changed. For some reason I can't imagine, he seems sad and unreachable. I try to lighten the atmosphere. 'Are you a vampire or something?'

'No, but I'm too old for you anyway.'

'You don't look a day over thirty.'

He laughs. It's a bitter sound. 'I'm thirty-two, but people like me, we're like meteorites. We don't last. We are bright, really bright, we can light up the sky with our fire, but we burn out and hurt the people around us. But I'm not going to harm you. I'm going to be gone long before I do that to you.'

I don't like the sound of that. For a strange reason it frightens me. I remind myself that we're just fucking. He has a girlfriend. I know nothing about him. I'm playing his mistress. And so far so good. I won't let him spoil it by talking about things that are outside our reach.

'What the fuck are you talking about, Jaron?'

It seems he's had enough of this strange talk too. 'No more talking, Billie love.'

The words Billie and love in the same sentence from his lips. So odd it is obviously a slip of the tongue.

'No more talking, Billie Black,' he corrects himself.

He takes me into a totally white bedroom. It is like a slice of heaven. There might be clouds under the bed. I know instantly that it is not his bedroom. He throws me on the white bed. The silk duvet is cold on my skin. I bounce and quickly raise myself on my elbows. He looks down at me with hooded eyes.

'This is not your bedroom, is it?'

'No.'

'Is this where you take the girls you...like?'

'No.'

'Why have you brought me here then?'

'Do you know you talk too much, Miss Black?'

'Why does every fucking thing have to be such a secret? Why can't you just be cool and tell me?'

'I can't have you and you can't have me. Why pretend?'

I sit up and cross my arms over my midriff. 'Just so we are clear, I don't want to marry you or anything like that. I'm quite happy to just think of you as the most enormous erection I have ever had the good fortune to come across. So stop being so fucking secretive. It's irritating.'

As if I had waved a magic wand the other Jaron, the smooth-talking operator, comes back. Un-fucking-believable. I stare at him in awe. What is he? A multiple personality. He looks me up and down so slowly my nipples tingle. 'You're a sight for sore eyes when you're irritated, babe,' he says very, very softly.

He bends and kisses me, but his kiss betrays him. It is not sexy. It is long and lingering and almost desperate. It reminds me of the way my grandfather grasped my hand when he knew he was dying. Like a claw. Even after he died his hand was tightly clenched around mine. I was so shocked I did not move. My mother came and disentangled his thin hand away.

'Where is he gone?' I asked.

'To heaven.' My mother sniffed.

'Is it a horrible place?' I asked.

'Of course not. It's a wonderful place. You only get to go there if you are good.'

'So why didn't he want to go then?'

My mother had no satisfactory answer for me. Why do we fear dying if heaven is waiting?

Jaron is looking at me with a crazy expression on his face. My lips form a single shivery word: 'Jaron?'

'I want you to take all of me,' he says roughly.

'OK,' I whisper. The idea is unfamiliar and exciting.

'Bum up,' he says, and lays me face down on the bed with two pillows under my hips. The thought of being taken from behind, of being face down, my ass high in the air and totally helpless, waiting for a *man* to mount me is, to my mind at least, dark and twisted.

He is the master of both our pleasures. His powerful hands run down my back and ass cheeks and down to the insides of my thighs. With both hands he opens me wide. That single rough action is the most erotic thing that has ever happened to me.

Suddenly there I am, spread open for his pleasure. Maybe if he wasn't such a hulk of a man or so brutishly muscular it wouldn't have caused the sensation of such powerlessness in me.

I am so wet and turned on that I groan when he enters me. I exhale slowly and savor the full, forbidden pleasure of having a man's dick inside me, a woman who thought she despised dicks. Perhaps he feels my excitement and how close I am to orgasm. My muscles are already beginning to spasm.

'Yes,' I scream.

The orgasm comes suddenly and powerfully but it lasts only a short time. My thighs are twitching and quivering, but he orders me not to move and takes me again and again. So hard that it makes him grunt and the bed shakes and the headboard rattles against the wall. His hands are on my hips, the fingers digging painfully into my flesh, and I am juddering about like a rag doll, but in my head I want him to grip me even harder, ravish me even more, brand me. I open my mouth and ask for it.

He doesn't disappoint. His thrusts build up even more speed. He is like a jackhammer inside me. I begin to tremble and then an orgasm tears through me. This one is really the one that sages talk about. It is like a death. It shreds you, lays you bare to all kinds of odd sensations. Floating. Out of body. Hues. Emotions. I cry when I come down and he holds me close.

'What's the matter?' he asks.

I shake my head, unable to speak.

'Did I hurt you?'

I shake my head again. This time I try to reassure him by holding his hand. He doesn't understand. He never will. He'll never know what I experienced.

He strokes my hair. 'I'm sorry,' he whispers.

'Don't,' I tell him. 'It was beautiful.'

'Really?' He seems stunned.

'It was insane.'

'Insane?'

'Out of this world,' I tell him.

He grins.

'Did you come?' I ask belatedly.

'Yeah. Did you not feel it?'

'Sorry. I was too lost in my sexual high.'

He is still inside me and I feel his cock twitch again. I know what that means. 'Can we rest a little?' I ask.

'Yeah,' he says and lies gently on top of me, but he remains inside me, semi-erect. I know the night is not over and for that I am insanely grateful.

'Do you have, like, a secret sexual fantasy?'

'Yeah, I have fantasies.'

'Something you'd be ashamed to share with anyone else?'

The blood rushes to my head. 'Yeah.'

His eyes glitter like jewels. Precious. Beautiful. Full of secrets. People have killed for them. 'What is it?'

Because I dare not look at the effect of my words on his face, I lift my head to his ear and whisper it.

Eight

A tinny, unfamiliar ringing wakes me up. Usually I need a police siren held to my head to wake me up, but being in a foreign bed with a man's body next to me makes me extra sensitive to my surroundings. I open my eyes and my fuzzy gaze falls on white walls, white carpets, white cupboards. For a crazy second I am confused. Where the hell am I? I turn my head the other way and my eyes suddenly focus. Jaron is lying on his front, his face turned to me. As I watch him, his eyes open and for a second he stares at me.

I am strangely embarrassed. 'Your phone's ringing.'

'Good morning.'

'Aren't you going to take it?'

'No.'

Immediately I suspect it is Ebony and I sit up and thrust my legs out of the bed. He catches my hand and tugs so I fall onto his body.

'Where do you think you're going?'

'Home.'

'It's not Ebony,' he says softly, his voice ultra-husky with sleep. 'You can look if you want.'

'No thanks,' I say, making my face blank so he cannot tell how I am reacting to his erection. I shift my weight, which only makes it worse.

He chuckles—the sound is warm and sexy. 'I love you like this. All hazy and tousled and blunt around the edges.'

'Why didn't you tell me that you were going to bring a salami into the bed with you?'

One corner of his mouth lifts, a lovely little half-smile that goes with the sunlight coming in through the open windows. 'I always bring breakfast with me.'

'I like my salami sliced,' I say.

And he starts to laugh. 'Oh, Billie. There is just no one like you.' He tucks a skein of hair behind my ear.

'You came inside me last night,' I accuse.

'I know, I'm sorry. I got carried away. I've never wanted to come inside a woman before. But I want to come inside you all the time, Billie. I want to fill that pussy of yours with hot spunk until you drip like a sponge.'

'Wow! Dirty talk before breakfast.'

He doesn't smile. There is raw lust in his eyes.

'I'll stop by a chemist on my way home and get a morning after pill.'

'Will you go on the pill?'

'Why, are you planning to fuck me long time?'

'Long enough.' And there is a tension to his voice that wasn't there before.

'That's chocolate to my ears,' I say lightly, but in fact, his words jar. The truth is, no matter how much I lie to him or to myself, I don't like to think that what we have has a time limit. Which, of course, I realize from a purely intellectual level is a contradiction. Everything in life has a time limit. Even things that seem to last are taken away at death.

I am always reminded of that photo I once saw of a woman and her friend who had rigged up a camera to take a picture of them standing against a waterfall. They are smiling into the camera and totally clueless that behind them by some freak of nature the waterfall has caused a wave that is about to engulf and kill them in seconds. That is most of us. We are smiling into the camera of our relationships. Just behind us, the wave: the end of it all.

'Are you sore this morning?' he asks, tracing his finger along the bridge of my nose.

'After last night? Do you have to ask?'

'Yup. It turns me on to hear you say it.'

'Yes, I'm sore. I feel as if I've had a sandstone pillar repeatedly thrust into me.'

He pulls me up by my armpits while I squeal and puts me astride on his penis. It is hot and hard. He looks hungrily at my breasts. 'Put me inside you.'

'I'm sore.'

'I want you to be more sore.'

I look into his eyes. They are heavy with desire. 'Why?' I whisper, but I have already lifted my hips and caught his large cock by its base.

'Because I want to brand you. All day long I want you to feel the pain and remember me inside you. I want you to be wet and ready by the time I come back tomorrow evening.'

I hold his shaft at the center of my core. 'Are you going somewhere tonight?'

'Yup.'

I sit on his cock and slide it all the way in. And boy does it stretch and burn.

'Pain?'

I nod.

'Good,' he growls.

I breathe out noisily.

'No cheating. I want to feel the lips of your pussy open and flatten around the base of my cock.'

I wriggle and push farther down. The action makes me gasp.

'Lean forward.'

Impaled on his shaft I lean forward and he squashes both my breasts together and sucks and bites both my nipples at the same time while I stretch my neck out and moan. It doesn't take long before both of us hit our highs. For the first time in unison.

I roll away from him and sit up. My toes sink deep into the luxurious carpet. 'I need a wash. I stink of sex.'

He catches my hand. 'Don't wash. I want you to be dripping my cum while we have breakfast. In fact, I don't want you to wash at all. All day long I want you to put your fingers between your legs, smell your fingers and remember my cock.'

I laugh.

'Show me your pussy.'

'What?'

'Open your legs and let me see your pussy.'

I look down at him, all messy hair and buffed. He is golden in the way only true blonds can be. An unrelievedly beautiful creature. The truth is I am a bit star-struck by him.

Slowly, I rotate my hips toward him and leaning back on the palms of my hands in the vague, probably futile hope that my stomach will stretch and look flatter than it really is, (there was a time I couldn't give a monkey's what anybody thought of my body but it is impossible to be like that when you are around someone as impossibly beautiful as Jaron) I smile slowly and open my legs.

'Fuck, Billie. That's beautiful.'

'What?' I ask innocently.

'My cum leaking out of you. Makes me want to fuck you all over again.'

'Forget that. I'm already burning.'

He puts his hand out and inserts a long finger into me. I inhale sharply.

'Does it hurt?'

'Like hell,' I reply and we are interrupted by a sound downstairs. I start and look at him questioningly.

He grins. 'Relax, that's only Ian, my housekeeper. Feel like breakfast?'

I take his finger out and close my legs. 'Yeah, but not eggs and bacon.'

'I know. A bowl of jam.'

I stare at him in disbelief. 'You've had me investigated?'

He links his hands behind his neck. Casual and unrepentant. 'I only wanted your address, but Drake was a bit more thorough than I expected.'

The phone rings again. He picks it up this time. 'Yeah, you can bring it up.'

He jackknifes into a sitting position and I am reminded again how agile and light he is considering his mountainous size. He stands and, naked, walks to a cupboard. He opens it, takes two fluffy toweling robes out and hands one to me. It is very large and I have to fold the sleeves.

'Come on,' he says and takes me up to the roof. A small, dapper man in a gray sweater and black trousers is already there. Jaron introduces him as Ian. Ian greets us both and starts to serve. I take the chair Ian holds out for me to sit on. Even though I have a balcony it has never crossed my mind to have breakfast in the fresh morning air. It's actually nice—very nice.

My bowl of jam is served to me on a silver tray with a teaspoon set next to it. Jaron is having the works—bacon, sausages, hash browns, eggs, beans and toast. After Ian disappears Jaron takes a sip of his orange juice and regards me over the rim of his glass. I put a spoon of jam into my mouth.

'I never would have believed it if I had not seen it,' he says.

'What?'

'Jam for breakfast. I thought Drake had finally cocked up.'

'Everybody makes such a fuss. I like jam. Why shouldn't I have it?'

'It's not exactly good for you.'

I have a few choice answers to that but I don't want to spoil a perfectly fine morning. Besides, he looks insanely fucking sexy in the morning light. 'So, tell me, what sort of business is it that you do? This place can't exactly be cheap.'

'What if I told you I'm an arms dealer?'

I look him dead in the eye. There is a tight, horrible feeling in my stomach. I'd rather he dealt in drugs. 'Are you?'

He chows down a piece of bacon dripping with the egg yolk: absolutely disgusting.

'No. I'm in property development.'

I exhale the breath I am holding. 'So what is it that you do then?'

'Did I not say? Property development.'

I nod. 'You must do very well.'

'I do OK.' He smiles. 'It pays the bills.'

'And you are trying to break into the fashion business,' he says, very smoothly changing the direction of our conversation.

'Drake is very thorough.' I spoon a mouthful of jam. 'I was curious about something. Why did you go to that dive where we met? I mean, you obviously don't take tainted Es and hardly drink...'

'I went there because I like the music.'

'And you never want to get high or drunk?' I ask him curiously.

'That's not how I get my high.' He takes his phone from the pocket of his dressing gown, hits a few buttons, scrolls through a list, and uses his index finger to click on something. 'Here,' he says passing his phone to me. 'Watch this.'

I take the phone from him and look at it. It looks like snow-covered terrain taken from the air. The angel changes and I realize that it has been taken from a helicopter. I can see its shadow on the snow.

'That's me wingsuit surfing a thousand feet over the highest mountain peak in the world, the summit of the Himalayas.'

The camera pulls back to a man standing at the door of the helicopter. He is wearing a blue helmet and it is impossible to see his face, but I can tell that he is Jaron. He simply drops out of the helicopter and the video shows him simply free falling against a blue sky. Shite. That looks fucking dangerous. Suddenly the feed changes back to one of those gopro cameras and it looks very much like Jaron is falling to his death on some snow-covered mountain called the Himalayas.

'That's me traveling at over one hundred miles per hour,' Jaron says.

The problem is no parachute opens and the mountain peak seems to be rushing up at frightening speed toward the camera. Involuntarily, I open my mouth. Is Jaron showing a video of him crashing into a mountainside? He is now so close to the ground I can even see tracks on the snow left by wild animals. Pull up, pull up, I want to shout.

'My God!' I exclaim.

'That happens fifteen feet from the ground.'

What he is referring to is the most amazing thing I have ever seen. The falling man suddenly flares out and becomes a human glider. His suit has wings. All in black he flies down the mountainside full of dark, sharp rocks and snow like that creature from the mothman prophesies. He flies over dangerously craggy rocks as if he is powered by something more than the webbed wings of his suit. The sense of space and drama is incredible. He looks no bigger than a fly, so vulnerable against one of the most hostile landscapes on earth. It almost doesn't look real. Surely humans can't do that! He flies so near the sharp rock I actually feel an odd prickle of fear and panic for him. It is only a video, I have to remind myself.

Then his blue parachute opens and he no longer flies like a bird, but looks like a helpless human being, tossed about by nature, flung down a mountainside. The parachute slows him down and he begins the motion of running while still airborne until he reaches a snowy patch where he lands and carries on running.

He stops running. The parachute around him. He is safe. And I look up at Jaron with totally different, totally impressed eyes. The nerves of steel required to free fall from that height and then to wait till fifteen feet off the ground before raising your arms to unfurl those puny little suit wings. Talk about the ultimate extreme sport.

'This is what you do to get a high?'

He chews and nods at the same time. 'Yeah. And sky diving, bouldering—'

'Bouldering?'

'Climbing without safety equipment.'

'That's just stupid.'

He shrugs and continues the list I interrupted. '...and volcano boarding.'

'What the hell is that?'

'It's zooming down the face of an active volcano on a reinforced plywood toboggan.'

'Ugh! What do you use for brakes?'

He grins. 'My heels.'

My mouth drops open. 'No shit! What sort of speeds do you do?'

'I've clocked speeds of nearly ninety kilometers per hour.'

'Right. So a helicopter drops you up there and you zoom down.'

'Nope.' He pours himself a cup of coffee. 'You have to hike up there first.'

I shake my head. 'Jesus, you're really intent on harming yourself, aren't you?'

He laughs. 'If you want you can come sky diving with me the day after tomorrow.'

'I won't be falling out on my own, will I?'

'Of course not. You'll be harnessed to me.'

'OK.'

Nine

I call Lana from the taxi.

'How was it last night?
'Absolutely fantastic.'
She laughs. 'Good. Shall we have lunch?'
'Royal China?'
'One o'clock.'
'You're bringing Sorab, right?'
'Of course.'
'Good. See ya later.'

By the time Lana arrives with my godson—
he's cuter than a six-week-old puppy—I am
already on my second glass of orange juice and
vodka.

'Sorry I'm late,' she apologizes. 'You look
amazing, by the way.'

But I don't really listen. Lana is always late.
I take Sorab in my arms and he smacks me
one straight on the mouth. I giggle because he
is actually a very serious baby. I guess he's like
his father. Hard to get him to crack a smile for
the most part. He has shiny bright eyes that
watch you carefully. Sometimes he looks at me
as if he is about to tell me off for smoking too
much or drinking in the morning or eating
stale pizza.

We settle him into his high chair with a
coloring book and a couple of sticks of crayons

and order our food. As soon as the waitress goes away with the menus Lana fixes me with her beautiful eyes. Did I ever tell you, my best friend is to die for gorgeous? When I was younger I fancied her something rotten. I might even have been a little in love with her. OK, OK, I was a lot in love with her. Me and a few other guys I know. I never told her, though. I thought it might make things awkward. Maybe one day I'll tell her and we'll laugh about it.

'So,' she says, leaning forward eagerly, her eyes inquisitive but warm, the way your best friend's eyes should be. 'Tell me about Mr. Pecs, Abs and Bulging Biceps, then.'

'Still throwing me against walls and ramming his cock into me.'

For a moment she looks surprised then she throws her head back and laughs. 'Oh, Billie. You are priceless.'

'No, really,' I say with a straight face. 'That is what he does. Fuck hard. All the time.'

Lana glances at her son. 'I'm going to have a lot of explaining to do if Sorab's first word is made up of four letters.'

I look at Sorab. He is scribbling furiously in his coloring book.

'I can't imagine why you wouldn't want him to learn such a versatile and useful word. It is the only word in the English language that serves as an adjective, a verb and a noun. Besides, I think it is really cute when babies swear.'

She looks unimpressed.

'You'll be telling me next you don't want Sorab to play with fire.'

She laughs and so do I. The sound comes easy. Life is wonderful. I think about Jaron. I want to remain cynical and detached, possibly even emotionally articulate, but I can't. It's like having a gift-wrapped Ferrari delivered to your door, and having someone say, 'Act cool.'

'So you're really into this guy, then?'

'Well, I'm still stuck on sixty-eight, but other than that all is just swell.'

'Sixty-eight?'

'He's gone down on me, but I still owe him one.'

Lana gasps at my directness and I wink at her.

Suddenly she smiles warmly. I'm not in love with her anymore but I do so love her. 'I'm so glad for you, Billie,' she says. 'I don't think I've ever seen you look so happy.'

'Don't go making any wedding plans yet,' I say dryly. 'The sex is out of this world fantastic and everything, but there's something not quite right about it all.'

'What do you mean?'

'He wears masks for different occasions. Sometimes I think I've seen the real him, but I'm not sure. The other night I was staring at him, looking into his moss green eyes, and suddenly I had this crazy thought. I wished I was a wolf. You know how they have enhanced senses. So every time he's anxious and sweating or lying I would hear his heartbeat change. How fucking crazy is that?'

'Are you in love with him, Bill?'

'No,' I say immediately. 'Of course not. He's a liar.'

'You said he has moss green eyes. When was the last time you looked that deeply into anybody's eyes?'

'I'm having sex with the guy. Obviously I'm going to look into his eyes.'

'Oh yeah? What was the color of your ex's eyes?'

'Blue.'

'Not sea blue, or light blue, or flame blue?'

I frown. 'Her eyes weren't her best feature.'

'I rest my case.'

'It's not love, OK? I'll admit that we do have some kind of strange connection. And while it is also true that I've never had it with anyone else, the relationship is not straightforward by any means.'

Lana immediately looks worried. 'What do you mean by that?'

'Well, he deliberately shrouds himself in mystery. He has defenses, strong defenses. He is like a castle with a moat around him. Every time I try to cross that moat he disarms me first with one of his wicked smiles and then we are thrashing around the room in the wildest sexual behavior imaginable and I have forgotten what I wanted to know until he is gone.'

I stop and take a large gulp of my drink. I feel hot and bothered. I wonder if they have turned up the heat in the place. Lana leans forward and takes my hand. She has a small, narrow hand with delicate fingers, the nails painted white. The difference between her hand and Jaron's is the difference between an elephant and a blueberry muffin: incalculable. It's strange how much I suddenly miss Jaron's large, powerful hand. I look up at her. She is frowning and full of protective instinct. God, I love this girl.

'Shall I ask Blake to check him out?' she offers.

For a second I am tempted. After all, he checked me out. He knew where I lived and that I have jam for breakfast. Who knows what else he knows? But the second passes. I don't want to check him out. I don't want to snoop around. I kinda respect him. I want him to have his privacy. Besides, if I find out something awful and I suspect I might do, I'd have to do something about it, and I'm not ready to do that yet. Let it just be liberated me having fun for a bit.

'No, I don't want him checked out,' I say.

'OK. But if ever you change your mind, just let me know. The things Blake can find out will blow your mind.'

'I don't want to find out things about him. I want to know what he thinks, but I don't want someone else to tell me. I want him to tell me.'

She smiles one of her Zen smiles. 'And he will.'

'What makes you say that?'

She pauses and bites her finger while she mulls something over in her head. She looks up as if she has made up her mind. 'I trust him. Yes, I would trust him if I were you.'

'Why?'

'I only met him once but I got good vibes from him. I liked him. In fact, let's all go out next week. I'd like to know him better.'

'OK.'

'We'll go to Annabel's. I'll watch him carefully.'

The thought of Lana watching Jaron closely makes me laugh.

'We are free on Wednesday and Thursday night. Ask him to choose a night.'

'Fine, I'll ask him tomorrow.'

'Why? Where is he now?'

'Monte Carlo.'

'Doing what?'

'I don't know and I don't want to know.' I sound rational and objective, but only I know that it is a total lie. I'd kill Bambi to know.

Our dumplings arrive and that thread of conversation is lost in the commotion of feeding Sorab, and tucking into lumps of unrecognizable meats stuffed into pretty shapes.

By the time we part it is nearly four o'clock. I take Sorab home with me. I feed him, mess about with him, then chuck him in the bath, and let him fall asleep in my lap. By eight thirty he is sound asleep in his cot and I sit and work until his parents come to pick him up at nearly midnight. Lana looks flushed. I know that look. I grin knowingly at her and she is such a little innocent she turns an even darker shade of red. I watch Blake pick up his sleeping son and for the first time in my life wonder if I will ever have children or a husband.

After they are gone, I feel strangely restless. I wonder what Jaron is doing and why he has not called. And always at the back of mind is the nagging question—why didn't he take me, has he taken Ebony?

I pull out my pack of cigarettes and go out onto the balcony. I like it out here. The view at night is always pretty. Sliding a cigarette between my lips I light it. I inhale deeply and let the warm, sharp smoke fill my lungs before I exchange it for cool night air. Peace should have surrounded me. But it is not peace. Every day with him another piece of me exposes itself. I am a jigsaw that even I do not know. I suddenly feel cold. I smooth my T. It's just sex, I tell myself. The more I fuck him the less I will want him. One day soon it will get old. I gaze at the dark sky and contemplate where he might be. What he could be doing. Who he could be fucking.

Fuck him, I think venomously. If he wants to fuck around let him. I don't give a shit anyway. We're not exclusive. I'm just having fun. And he is fun. For no apparent reason an image of Ebony's two-inch talons curled around Jaron's massive dick flashes into my mind and I actually feel physically sick. I stand from the couch. She must shred her vagina to ribbons every time she uses a tampon, I think bitchily. But the awful feeling of jealousy doesn't pass.

I switch the TV on, take down the bottle of vodka and start drinking alone, and after a while I feel nicely warm and fuzzy. I switch off the TV. It was doing my head in anyway. Immediately my mind reverts to Jaron.

'I don't want...' I start saying aloud and then I catch myself on the verge of a confused, drunken confession to thin air.

'Better go to bed,' I mutter and stagger toward the bedroom. The balcony door is open but I am too lazy to stumble over there and mess about with the sliding lock. It's a safe area. There are never any robberies around here. None that I know of, anyway.

I brush my teeth and catch my own reflection. I look pale. 'Who's with you tonight?' Fucking cheating snake. I stumble into the bedroom and fall into bed feeling furious and impotent. I really should have closed the balcony door. My last thought is... Bastard.

Ten

I'm pulled abruptly from a deep, alcohol-fueled sleep. My body feels like lead, I can barely open my eyes, but the fear is immediate. Something is wrong. Like an animal I smell the danger. I didn't close the balcony door.

Someone is on my bed!

My eyes jerk open. It is too dark to see. I'm being turned over as though I'm weightless. I open my mouth to scream and something soft is stuffed into my mouth. My body goes into shock and I freeze. During those precious moments of inaction the man straddles my body on my thighs and pins my arms down and over my head.

I start struggling.

But he already has the upper hand and he does nothing, only stays motionless and watches my useless struggles. My brain suddenly understands. He is just trying to tire me. I immediately cease struggling. My whole body is trembling violently with fear. I try to speak around the gag, but only strange guttural sounds escape.

'Shut the fuck up...' he says, and pulls both my hands together and, trapping them with just one hand, takes his other hand into my nightgown. He touches me between my legs. I shudder with fear and horror.

Roughly, he tears away the scrap of material between him and me and I start screaming my lungs out, but the sounds that come out will not carry. They are muffled and grunt-like.

I try to pull my thighs together, but it is impossible because he is sitting on them. Enjoying my total helplessness, he lifts himself momentarily to part my legs farther and I take that opportunity. With a burst of sudden strength I roll to the other side of the bed and spring out.

My only thought is escape.

I run toward the door. I know I won't make it to the front door and then try to mess around with the locks. If I can just get to the kitchen I can grab a knife. He bolts after me. I can hear him.

I am at the dining table when he captures my upper arms and whirls me around to face him. He presses my body against him and catches my wrists and holds my hands high above my head. I'm not a black belt in judo or anything but I do know exactly how to disengage a man. I bring my knees upward but he pushes his hips back so I miss him, lose balance and stagger. He twirls me around.

He has the advantage of brute strength, but it is so dark in the dining room with all the curtains pulled shut that it is very hard to make anything out. That is my advantage. I know my house far better than he.

I lunge suddenly for the large, antique bronze clock that Lana bought for me and heave it toward me. The weight of it makes me collapse in a heap, the clock hitting the floor with an almighty crash. The thunder of its crash is obscene in the terrible silence of our struggle.

The silhouette falls on top of me and curls his hands around my throat and starts choking. A whisper, chillingly close, says, 'Do not move.'

On my hands and knees, I freeze. He stops choking me. The ticking of the clock becomes so loud, I need to distract him. I let out the breath I am holding.

The clock is still gripped hard in my hands. I know I don't have the strength to swing the clock but if I turn around suddenly I can smash my heel into his jaw. I feel a surge of adrenalin.

'You should not have run. You should have accepted your fate...in your bed.'

I turn my head slowly in the direction of his voice. He is masked. A frighteningly white mask. It gleams in the gloom. I cannot breathe for the gag. He does not want money. I have only one thought in my head. *I must find some way...*

The man tilts his head. 'I have a knife.'

I make a small begging sound.

He fists my hair and lifts my face off the floor. 'You are going to be raped.'

In an instant I grasp the true horror of my situation. I am totally helpless.

'No!' I scream, summoning all my strength. He pins me down with his body. Then every sound becomes amplified a thousand times in my head. A trouser zip being undone. The white mask falls close to my face. Before I can look up a blindfold is put over my eyes and tied behind my head. He doesn't want me to see his face, to call out, spoil his fun. Never before have I been blindfolded and gagged in the dark. I thrash out with my hands and he bites my shoulder. The pain makes me cry out but it also forces me to submit to his greater force. I am his captive. The more I struggle the more I am going to be hurt.

He presses his hand down on my back just below my shoulder and pulls my T-shirt nightie from under me. He tears it in two and exposes my buttocks and my back. I close my eyes when I feel his hard shaft released and pressing on the small of my back. I can smell him now. A man's smell. Raw. A mixture of sweat and leather. The gag in my mouth is wet with my saliva.

Quickly he clasps his strong forearms around my waist and hoists my ass in the air, before parting my legs forcefully. Wasting no time, a massive cock is being forced inside me with such violence that I feel it tear me as it just keeps feeding into me, mercilessly stretching and going deeper and deeper, reaching right into my womb. I grunt when it finally can go no farther. There is a button or zipper caught between me and his body that scratches my thigh every time he moves. I block it out.

Then the pummeling begins.

He rides me relentlessly with brute force. I feel his sweat dripping onto my naked skin. He reminds me of an express train that is out of control. I am driven into so hard and fast that I cannot stop myself from being aroused in spite of myself. From wanting it. From moaning. From climaxing.

Over and over.

His huge cock, throbbing, pulsating inside me suddenly shoots a hot stream up deep into my sex and his bulk collapses on top of me. We are both panting hard. My body is trembling, my sex still quivering with the pounding it has just received. He rolls off me easily and lies beside me, facing the ceiling.

'Is that what you wanted?' he asks.

I turn over so I too am facing the ceiling. 'You ought to be careful. I was going to stab you with a kitchen knife.'

He chuckles. 'Is that how you reward someone who brings your most secret fantasy to life?'

I turn to my side and kiss him on the lips. 'Thank you. That is one hell of a fuck. I will never forget that one. I loved being raped by you.'

'When did you know it was me?'

'One second after I woke up, but it was fun to pretend.'

'I brought something for you,' he says softly.

'Is it small and expensive?' I joke, to cover my surprise and elation that he has thought of me while he was away and bought me something.

'Yeah,' he says and switches on a table lamp. I blink in the sudden glare. With a smug look he straps a bracelet on my wrist.

I lift my wrist and look at it. Even in the dim light of the lampshade it shimmers like blue fire. 'Jesus. Is it real?' I gasp.

'Of course.'

'My God.' I exclaim, and sitting up stare at my wrist in shock. 'It's...stunning.' I turn to look at him.

He smiles indulgently. So this is what mistresses the world over feel. They get showered with pretty stones by men wearing indulgent expressions. It might bore me later but at this moment I can see the attraction of the job.

'I want to say you shouldn't have, but I can't, because I fucking love it.' I throw my arms around him and whoop with joy. Holding aloft my hand, I admire it. I pull away from his neck. 'What kind of stones are these?'

'Blue diamonds.'

'Oh, Lana has a pink diamond that cost the earth itself, but I've never seen a blue diamond before.'

'Now you have.'

'Oh, darling. I could so fall in love with you, when you behave like this,' I quip. It's a joke, obviously, but it doesn't come out right.

Eleven

This is the day of my first skydive. I wake up excited and the feeling does not go away until he walks through the door.

'Hey,' I say.

'You ready?'

'Yeah.'

'Scared?'

'Are you?'

'Me?'

'Yeah, you.'

'I'm not like anybody you know, Billie. I don't get scared of danger. I get excited.'

We stare at each other. Every day I become more and more intrigued by him.

'Let's go then,' I say.

When we get downstairs Jaron steers me toward a Pagani Huayra with gulf wing doors. I stop suddenly.

'Is that yours?' I ask in a shocked tone.

'Last time I looked, yeah.'

'Wow!' I squeal, running my eyes over the aluminum and glass trimmings. 'I *love* this baby.'

He chuckles. 'Its name means god of the winds in Quechua.'

'And why haven't you told me about this car before?' I demand aggressively as I start walking toward it.

He clicks his remote and the wings go out and up.

'Whoa,' I cry with serious admiration, and dash toward the driver's seat. He pulls me back by my jacket. I turn around and look at him enquiringly.

'You're in the passenger seat,' he says with his eyebrows raised.

'Can I at least drive on the way back?'

'Maybe. Let's see how you feel after your jump.'

'OK,' I agree, and slide into the plush leather seat, as happy as I have ever been in my life. 'I always saw you as an all black McLaren P1 guy.'

He glances at me curiously. 'Why?'

'I don't know, but I was wrong. This actually suits you perfectly.'

As soon as we hit the motorway Jaron puts his foot on the accelerator and the car zooms forward so fast I actually feel a knot of fear and excitement in my belly. No wonder he didn't want me to drive, if this is what he calls driving. We fly along, tearing past the rolling countryside until we turn off at the road leading to the airfield.

Jaron hauls our equipment out of the car and we go into the low building. He is well known there and so I am in a large locker room kitting myself out in a jumpsuit that goes over my clothes, gloves, goggles, and a helmet. Next is the harness. I step into it and Jaron pulls it up over my shoulders, and tightens all the straps to make it nice and secure. He checks it.

'All right?'

'A OK,' I say although a whole swarm of butterflies has invaded my belly at the thought that soon I will be jumping out of a plane.

'OK, face down on the floor,' he says.

'What do you mean?'

'I'll show you what position to free fall in.'

I lie on the floor, and he tells me to bend my legs at the knee and lift them about six inches in the air. We practice a few more moves and Jaron straps on his parachute.

'Ready to skydive?'

'Yikes,' I joke, but by now I am a jumpsuit of nerves. We walk over to the plane. I shuffle along and sit on the bench. Jaron waves to the pilot and shows the thumbs up signal. The plane taxies off and Jaron turns to me and attaches our harnesses together, tightening all the straps again to be certain that they are all safe and secure. For the next fifteen minutes while we ascend to jumping height, Jaron seems very calm and relaxed, and that helps a lot, but it is still a really strange feeling. I trust Jaron implicitly, especially after having seen the video, and for some weird reason I love the idea of having my fate tied so irrevocably with his. Also the way he has his large, gloved hand on my knee is dead protective and I am getting off on that. We clear the clouds at nine thousand feet.

'OK, thirteen thousand feet,' Jaron says.

'Time to jump?'

'Yeah,' and there is a frisson of exhilaration in his voice.

I look at him in wonder. So this is what he does for kicks.

'Get your goggles and helmet on,' he says, and I obey. I look out of the window and the jarring thought is: What the flying fuck am I doing? I have seen videos of jumpers falling out from planes and disappearing from sight and now it is my turn. Jaron shuffles me over to the edge of the plane, with our legs dangling out. My mind goes blank. And suddenly there is neither fear nor nervousness. A strange calm comes upon me. I turn my head to look up at Jaron. There is a strange light of excitement in his eyes. Our gazes meet and for a second we are connected on a deep level.

'Three...two...one, we jump.'

The force of the wind slams into me instantly as we hurtle through the sky at crazy speed. It pulls and sucks at the flesh on my face with a force that is shocking. My mouth drops open with the impact of the free fall and Jaron has to reach down and close it for me. I quickly get into the position Jaron taught me. The cold dry air and my own nervousness make my lips stick to my gums.

I bring my tongue out to wet my lips and my tongue is buffeted by the freezing cold wind. There are sharp ice droplets in the air and Jaron holds his hands out over my face to protect me. We fall at over a hundred miles per hour from thirteen thousand feet. I give in to the unique high of rushing through cold, clear air, the dip in the stomach. The speed and the sensation of danger push everything else out of my mind. It is unexplainable and amazing and so different from anything I have ever experienced. Never have I felt that sensation of all my senses being open, on alert and on edge.

The free fall lasts just under a minute.

At five thousand feet Jaron gives me the hand signal and I move my arms across my chest in the brace position and wait for him to pull the chute. As he pulls it we are dragged into a vertical position. In movies it always seems as if pulling the chute causes the person to jolt upwards with great force, but it does not happen like that. The parachute opens slowly and the fall in speed is gradual.

We begin to glide down under the canopy. Now that we can hear each other speak, Jaron asks, 'You all right?'

'Definitely,' I say, and I am filled with an odd emotion. A feeling of great tenderness for him. I don't exactly want to call it love, but it is protective and slightly possessive and full of gratitude for the experience we have just shared. He even lets me steer at one point.

He points to landmarks and I let my eyes follow his gloved hand, but I am still in a state of shock. My heart is pounding like a mad thing. It takes us four, maybe five minutes to glide down and then it is time to land. It was over too quick.

Jaron reminds me to raise my legs up. I immediately obey so I don't get injured. We have the perfect landing.

'Whoop... Touchdown, baby,' I holler.

Jaron unstraps me, and, turning me around, kisses me hard. Really hard.

'What was that for?' I ask, when he raises his head.

For a hot minute it seems as though he is going to say something important. Then he shakes his head and says, 'For coming with me and being so cool up there.'

I am buzzing like crazy. I grab his face and kiss him back passionately.

'What was that for?' he asks.

I want to tell him about that strange emotion I experienced about him in the air, but I stop myself.

'Thank you for that experience. It was super amazing,' I say excitedly. 'I shall never forget it.'

He nods.

I laugh with exhilaration. 'Can we go up again?'

He laughs too. 'Maybe not today.'

'God! It's the best drug in the world.' Adrenalin-fueled I whoop with joy. Finally, I understand one tiny part of him. That part of him that seeks out danger.

Twelve

We go to Lana and Blake's house and Tom, their chauffeur, takes us all to a private club called Annabel's.

The doormen usher us in like royalty and we end up at a red lacquered bar surrounded by artwork. The walls have depressing, old-fashioned, polished brass and dark oak panels, and the ceilings are low and Moorish. The lighting is kept so dim that there is the feeling of being in a tomb or a cave. The clientele represents the denizens of British aristocracy in suits and international men of mystery who have as decorative objects tall and stunning Eastern European women half their age, and of course the super rich spoilt children of the Middle Eastern oil men. The dress code is strict and everyone is in a suit or a cocktail dress. Despite every effort to retain a décor of the dark and somber appeal of a library, the atmosphere borders on the nouveau riche.

A few very expensive cocktails later we move to their dining room where the walls are lined only with bottles of Bordeaux. The maître d' does the usual and swarms all over Blake. The other waiters, mostly Italian, are friendly, a little cheeky and indulgent. We dine on some kind of Franco-Italian food, which is very good. Both Lana and I have pasta, Jaron orders the Bellota Iberica ham and Blake goes for blood-soaked steak. For starters Blake orders caviar, which is disgusting, but which everyone else seems to think is great. The wine is vintage and very expensive, but I don't like wine so I stick with my cocktails.

Blake is sophisticated and urbane, Lana sparkles, Jaron is charming and attentive, and I just watch Jaron. There is a dynamic at work that I don't understand. I watch Jaron work Blake Law Barrington and his wife. He is smooth. He is clever. He is funny. He is charming. And he is not the Jaron Rose I know. He is wearing a mask. He takes my hand, he looks into my eyes, he even leans in and kisses me on the lips, but this is not the Jaron I know.

The Jaron I know is assertive and demanding and, well, a fucking animal. This smooth, well-oiled...salesman is a shock to my system. Looking at him you'd never imagine that he flies down mountainsides in a wingsuit or goes to dive clubs where everybody is high on drugs just for the music. Is he hoping to get some business from Blake Law Barrington?

After bitter chocolate ice cream Lana and I move to the starlit dance floor to dance to cheesy seventies and eighties tracks. Obviously, I am conscious that I am dancing to ABBA but I have drunk so many fifteen pound cocktails I don't care anymore. It turns out to be surprisingly fun.

For the most part it is Lana and me who keep rushing off to the dance floor to boogie while the men stay and talk about whatever it is that men talk about when their women go off to the dance floor. Once they come to interrupt us. From the corner of my eye I see Blake whirl Lana away by the waist and hear her surprised, delighted laughter, and then I am distracted by a hand grabbing me by the ass and pulling me around.

'Classy, very classy,' I shout over the music.

'Don't give out all your compliments in one night,' he tells me and slams me into his body. I curl my hands around his neck.

'Are you having a good time?' I ask.

'Yeah, you were right. Blake is a great guy, for a billionaire.'

And I am filled with a sense of great relief. I think I had been worried that he would not get on with Blake. 'I wouldn't want to have him as my enemy, that's for sure. But it's great when he's married to your best friend.'

He replies but I don't catch it because *Mambo No. 5* comes on and I shout, 'Look, Jaron, they're playing your song.'

'Very funny,' he says, but we have a good time, with me kicking up my heels, singing, 'A little bit of Monica in my life, A little bit of Erica by my side, A little bit of Sandra in the sun. A little bit of you all night long makes me your man.'

Jaron twirls me around beautifully.

'Mambo number 5,' I scream, taking one step to the left and then one step to the right. Then we are clapping our hands twice in unison with all the other dancers while moving along and laughing.

'All we need now is a dose of *Macarena*,' Jaron says.

And shock horror, the DJ puts on *Macarena*. My mouth drops open. And then we fall about laughing. Jaron makes an exaggerated production of limbering up before following me in the Macarena dance. It's fun. I never expected him to be such a sport, to allow himself to be so goofy. Even Blake has a go. Lana looks flushed and happy and I wonder if I look like that too, because that is exactly how I feel inside. Flushed and happy.

By the time we get home it is nearly two in the morning and I am singing *Hips Don't Lie* by Shakira. 'No fighting, no fighting,' I sing tunelessly as Jaron stuffs me through the front door.

'Oh, baby, when you talk like that...'

He drags me to the bedroom, throws me on the bed and falls on top of me.

'My hips don't lie,' I tell him slowly, enunciating the words properly. 'I bought them in Columbia.'

He rolls me over so I am on top of him and it is immediately obvious that he is in no mood to banter. My knickers are sliding down my legs.

'You're mine,' he says harshly, so different from the man who sat at the dinner table at Annabel's. This is the Jaron I know. The promise in his words shivers straight to my sex.

'Do whatever you want to me,' I whisper hoarsely.

'Say it. Say you are mine.'

'I'm yours, Goldilocks. I'm all yours.'

'Now fucking ride me until you get home.'

I murmur something incoherent and start unbuckling his belt. I slide my wet pussy against his cock and adjusting it to the center of my core, push down. This drunken sex is beyond delicious. It is like part sex, part dream. It could become part misery if I am not careful: shit, where did that thought come from?

I blank it out immediately.

I shudder on the edge. 'Hell, I'm going to come,' I gasp and look into his face. His eyes are burning green and a thin sheen of sweat is making his skin glow. My heart trembles. Jesus, save me, I am falling for Goldilocks. And then I am going out with the waves that come to fetch me. The thin sheen of sweat on his body—I slip on it. Shit, am I falling for Goldilocks?

Thirteen

It starts innocuously. We are at an old haunt of mine, a gay club, and I say, 'I don't know what I am anymore.'

'You're a recovering lesbian,' he replies.

The glib answer irritates me and I decide to punish him. A little. 'I'm kinda missing the feel of soft skin,' I say.

An expression crosses his face. I can't say for sure what it is, but he quickly veils it. 'You want to bring another woman into bed with us?'

The question throws me. I had not actually thought that far, but now that he has said it I can't dismiss it either. 'I don't know,' I answer truthfully.

'Only one way to find out.'

I stare at him.

'Pick a woman you want and we'll ménage.'

'Have you been with two women before?'

'Of course.'

'Fun?'

He shrugs noncommittally. 'It was OK.'

I chuck back my vodka. 'All right, let's find out where I stand with this bisexual lark. Don't go far. I'll be back.'

He lifts his glass to his lips, his eyes utterly veiled. 'Good luck.'

Vodka is singing in my veins. I walk over to the bar. There is a girl I know standing at it. She is actually very beautiful with long dark hair and she has a stud in her belly button. I know because I have been to bed with her.

'Billie,' she says.

'Sahara,' I say.

She kisses me on the lips and introduces me to two other friends of hers. Both have just come back from the dance floor with sheens of sweat on their faces. One is a butch girl called Gerry, and the other is a truly stunning half-caste girl with light eyes. Impossible to tell the color in the dark. Her lips are big and delicious-looking. Her name is Poppy. Lovely. Poppy trails her soft chocolate finger on my bare skin. Honestly, black girls have the softest skin of all races. Like baby skin. I knew straight away I could have invited her over. I could have had her.

But I turn away from her and smile at Gerry. Big, spiky-haired, poor, ugly Gerry. She smiles back, eyes shining.

'Where did you get your tats done?' she asks.

For a pick-up line it sucks miserably. 'Kilburn,' I tell her.

'They're nice,' she lies lamely. Chocolate finger was better. By far better. Still. I guess she'll do for tonight.

And then I stop myself.

Who am I fooling? I know exactly why I am not picking the real beauty of the bunch. I don't want Jaron to be interested in her. I can't bear the thought of him being sexually attracted to another woman.

I think about all their clever pussy muscles clenching and releasing my fingers as I make them come, and yes, intellectually it is a hot thought, but my stomach doesn't quake. Not even the thought of their tongues licking my clit does it. I turn and look across the room at Jaron. He is looking down at the table and he seems unreachable and...for that moment maybe even sad. I stare at him.

'Got to go. I'll call you,' I tell Sahara. I wink at Poppy (lovely girl) and shrug at Gerry.

I walk back to the table. At a pillar I stop and watch him.

In the light of the nightclub his hair stands out. Blond men are a rare thing. He is wearing black leather trousers that hug his hips and gleam under the nightclub lights. He sits at the table, cool, relaxed. And I have to admit he is drastically sexy. I watch him flick a glance at the dance floor and get distracted by a woman in a bikini top and a nothing skirt.

She is beckoning to him with one finger. Bitch! The flare of jealousy and irritation is instant and burns at my guts. I quell the desire to stalk up to her and ram her finger down her throat. I stare at Jaron. He extends his thumb and last finger and bends all the fingers between and holds his hand as if it is a receiver to his face. What the fuck? He knows someone in my old haunt? A gay club? And the fucking bastard wants her to call him.

I stalk up to him. 'Who was that?'

'Gemma.'

'Gemma?' I can't help how sharp my voice sounds.

He breaks into an idiotic smile. 'You're jealous?'

'No. I am not fucking jealous.'

'Then it's no problem.'

'Can I ask you a stupid question anyway?'

'Fire away.'

'Are you sleeping with her too?'

'Why would you think that?'

That answer inflames me beyond all reason. I want to go around and slap him. I am in a bad way for this guy. And he is so cool and unconcerned and so fucking unavailable. 'Just once can you just answer the fucking question?' I grit.

He laughs deep and dark. I realize then that there will always be about him an undercurrent of lurking danger. Like a deep, deep well. 'No,' he says very clearly. 'I'm sleeping with you.'

'So what are you asking her to call you for?'

'She works for a friend. I want you.' His voice is tense and low. 'Exclusively. If you want to bring another woman into the picture and share me it's your call, but I'm not sharing you with anyone else. If I see a man even sniffing the air around you, I'll rip his skin off.'

The breath squashes from my lungs.

Jaron is watching me, his eyes deliberately blank. 'Well?' he asks.

I make up my mind pretty quick. 'Come on,' I say, and pull him off his chair.

He slides off easily and follows me out of the nightclub. I'll give him this. The guy knows when not to chatter. Never asks me where we are going. Simply follows. I like that. I turn down the road and into a side street. I know this place. I came here once to vomit. It leads to a cobblestone alleyway. There are large silver wheelie bins and black bin bags of rubbish stacked by them.

I pull him into the shadows of a doorway and slam him against the door. The sound is loud in the deserted place.

'Remember when I said, I'd *never* suck your dick?'

'You changed your mind?' He chuckles.

'You're a genius, Jaron Rose,' I say and start unzipping his pants. He is as hard and as long as a policeman's baton.

'I have a crazy fantasy. In it I am a policewoman who stops a very attractive woman on a deserted road. "Did I do something wrong, Officer?" she simpers. "You were speeding," I tell her firmly, taking out my ticket book. "You're not going to give me a ticket, are you?" she asks alarmed. "I'm afraid so, lass," I say opening my book. "I'm so very sorry, Officer," she purrs. "I promise to be more careful next time." I click the top of my pen. "Surely there must be something I can do for you?" she asks desperately.'

Jaron's face is a picture. He is so turned on his jaws are clenched. I reach into his black boxers and take out his baton in my hand. It twitches with excitement.

'"Maybe," I inform the young lady. Then I make her get out of the car and tell her very, very sternly to bend over the car hood with her legs spread open. In my fantasy the dirty girl is not wearing any knickers. I lay my palm on her lily-white buttocks and slowly push my baton into her wet, wet pussy. She screams with pleasure.'

At that moment I drop to my knees on the cold cobblestones and move my mouth toward his cock and the smell of his leather trousers. With my eyes trained on him I slowly push the thick shaft between the nice, tight O of my lips. He tastes nothing like I thought he would. Spice and plums! I don't eat plums and I hate spicy stuff, but I like the taste of him.

His head rears back. 'Oh God!' he groans and I see the muscles of his hands bunch as they move toward my hair as if he wants to grasp it and control my head like he would the reins of a horse, but he stops himself in time. Maybe he doesn't want to scare me away. I open my throat and take him deeper and deeper into my mouth.

He looks down on me, his lust-filled eyes astonished by my skill. 'I love watching my cock fill your mouth,' he snarls.

He doesn't know that Lana and I have been to classes in London where we learned how to deep throat with a condom-covered banana. I am forced further down the trunk of Jaron's throbbing monster. His helmet pushes my tonsils aside and I gag as the silky head lodges at the base of my throat. For a few seconds the gag reflex sets in and I stop. My throat flutters desperately. I grip his knees hard.

'Sorry,' he says. 'But gag reflex just feels so fucking good.'

I don't like the sensation of gag reflex one little bit. I jiggle my tongue and gasp for air and then I remember. Just stop and it will pass. I wait and it passes and then I take him deeper past the back of my throat. Strange feeling. It's just like swallowing a sword, only his shaft is warm and round and satin soft. I take it all in.

'Suck my big, hard dick, baby. Suck it for me.' His voice is thick: a guttural growl.

I swirl my tongue against the thick pillar of meat and suck it the way I would have sucked a red ice lolly as a child. Greedily. Until it was white ice. He thrusts his hips. I let him hold my head and fuck my mouth. When his climax begins to shudder through his body he warns me to pull away.

'Otherwise I'm coming in your mouth,' he rasps as his knees buckle.

But I don't disengage. Instead I grab his hips and pull them toward me, my lips wrapped tightly around his girth.

He grabs my hair and his hips carry on fucking my mouth until he explodes so deep in my throat I don't taste his semen. He inhales sharply and lets loose another throatful of thick, hot cum.

He pulls me to my feet, his cock still semi-hard, and looks into my eyes. His eyes are glittering. 'What the fuck, Billie? You did that like a fucking pro.'

'I was making up for the fact that you're never going to have a threesome with me.'

He looks at me quizzically. 'I didn't want a threesome with you.'

'Good because you're not getting it.'

'I thought you wanted it.'

'I don't,' I say belligerently.

'That was the best blowjob I've ever had.'

I grin. 'Bet my breath stinks of sperm.'

'Wish you always stank like that.'

'Whoa.'

'Where on earth did you learn to give head like that anyway?'

'London,' I say airily.

The sinfully sexy dimple on his left cheek appears suddenly, deep and delicious. 'And what does the policewoman do after she has fucked the poor girl with her baton on the bonnet?'

'What's it to you?'

'I've got a baton.'

I look down at his cock. It is nearly hard enough to go again. 'And you've always wanted to be a very butch policewoman?' I ask.

A sly smile curves his lips as he runs one long finger down my cheek. Desire is radiating off him like sultry summer heat. The man is sex on a stick. He is the master of temptation. A shiver fishtails down my spine. He makes me want things I have never wanted. 'Don't let your imagination limit you, Ms. Black.'

I grin. 'I'm trying not to.'

He comes very close to me. I smell his skin, feel the heat of his hard male body. He licks my collarbone. 'Try harder.'

I swallow hard. 'She gets on her knees, opens the girl's bum cheeks and sucks her pussy dry.'

The dimple appears again, but this time his eyes are not laughing. They are dark and dangerous. When he is like this I feel as if I don't know him at all. What I see is only the mask. What lies underneath is different. Murky. He folds his hands over his chest. 'Take your panties off.'

I pull them off me hurriedly and drop them on the gritty stones.

His strong hand grabs mine and whirls me around so fast I feel almost dizzy.

'Place your hands on the wall where I can see them.'

I don't need to be told a second time. I *want* to be on the other side. The receiving side. My mind whirls with exhilaration and my flesh throbs as I place my palms on the rough bricks above my head and spread my legs wide. I close my eyes and invisible strings of compulsion race along my nerves. He is the policewoman with the baton. Sweat trickles down my spine. He slides his hand along the inside of my right thigh and suddenly thrusts his fingers forcefully into me.

I whimper. 'No, not that. I'm too close to the edge.' And I am not lying. I am so turned on I feel as if I could come at any time. The smallest little thing would make me come.

He grabs my hips and slides the thick, hot baton so deep into me that my head pulls back. Even before I can take a steadying breath he pulls out and slams back into me, but so brutally that I come with that second fucking thrust! And it is a savage orgasm. I cry out in ecstasy as wave after wave hits me hard. He freezes. The odd echo of my scream dies and he turns me around and looks deep into my eyes. In the shadows of the alleyway where people only come to piss or vomit I have experienced energy racing inside me like quicksilver, connections and tremendous pleasure. My scalp is tingling, heart is pounding hard and my knees are trembling. This must be what they call fantastic sex.

'Did you just come?'

I am still in shock with how fast that tsunami was upon me. 'Crude but effective,' I croak.

'Wow!' he says wonderingly. 'You made that too easy. I'm nowhere near finished,' he says.

My need for him is feral, animalistic and insatiable. 'Let's go home. I want to lie spread-eagled on the dining table while you fuck me. So hard I feel you are ripping me open.'

For a while he stares at me. Then he nibbles and kisses my neck and says, 'You're coming with me tomorrow to my island.'

Fourteen

'There she is,' Jaron says. 'All nine and a half acres of her.'

I look out of the window of the seaplane and see a tiny teardrop-shaped island sparkling like a watermelon tourmaline in the hot blue sea. Surrounded by a thin border of white sand it has to be one of the most beautiful things I have ever seen and it is also love at first sight for me.

'Wow!' I exclaim. 'How very lucky you are.'

'Yes, I am very lucky to have her,' he shouts over the noise of the plane.

The little plane lands on the water, skimming it like a stone thrown on a lake, and taxies closer to the beach. As soon as it comes to a stop, I don't wait for the men standing at the wooden pier to come get us by boat, I open the door and throw myself into the water, clothes, shoes and all. I hit the warm water with a splash and a great whoop of joy. I turn on my back and Jaron is looking at me with amusement.

'Come in,' I call.

He shakes his head. 'Thanks, but I'll pass.'

I swim lazily in the silky water while he goes on to the beach and meets three men who are waiting on the pier. From this far away I can't see their features, but one of them has long dreadlocks that have been bleached to a coppery color by the sun. They wear colorful clothes. Even from where I am I can see that their bodies are toned and muscular and their skins shine like highly polished wood.

They shake hands with Jaron and then they all turn to look at me. I wave at them, they wave back and then they all go back into the house with our luggage. The men, Jaron has told me, don't live on the island, and when they return to the mainland Jaron and I will be totally alone on this paradise island.

I kick my sandals off and get out of my heavy, clinging top and trousers. It is strangely liberating to watch them sink. Then I turn around and float dreamily on my back. The sky is blue in a way that it never is in England. A lone seagull high up circles and cries. The fierce sun beats on my face, but there is a cool breeze and the waves lap gently against my relaxed, drifting body. I feel almost hypnotized.

God! This is the life. I could just eat coconuts and stay here forever. I think of Jaron telling me that the motto of island life is: Take your time. No hurry.

Time passes.

'Hey,' someone calls. Reluctantly I right myself and tread water. Jaron is standing at the water's edge a little away from the pier. He is shading his eyes with his hands and not wearing shoes or a shirt.

'Want some lunch?' he shouts.

Food? Brilliant idea. Come to think of it I am actually starving hungry. 'Yeah, I do.'

'Come on then.'

I start swimming toward him. When I can feel the sand under my feet I start walking toward him. My limbs feel strangely heavy and lethargic. I look at Jaron and he is staring at me with hungry eyes. Must be the heat, but I feel as if there is a powerful coil of need inside me. A powerful desire to fall on him on the beach. The sun is hot on my head and the ground is the softest, whitest, most pristine, fine sand I've ever had the pleasure of walking upon. I walk up to him and stop a foot away.

We stare at one another, each mesmerized by the other. He reaches out a hand and glides his finger along my wet cheek. His skin is hot and his touch births a yearning inside me, something new. Something I have never felt before. I feel my cheeks blazing. The air around us shimmers. I look enquiringly into his eyes. But they are fierce wells of green fire that are devoid of any information. I have the impression that my body is on fire. I shake my head slightly. Confused, dazed by the sun. Perhaps it is some sort of heatstroke. I shouldn't have lain in the midday sun without easing myself into it slowly.

He leans in, catches my face in his hands and lightly brushes his lips against mine. The disconnect between the naked lust in his eyes and the tenderness of his lips disarms me. And suddenly the thought—I'm in love with this man. I am totally, completely and terribly in love with him. The knowledge is like freezing wind on my wet skin. I shiver. *Back up, Billie. Back up.*

I say the first thing that comes into my head. 'Did you say something about lunch?' My voice is croaky and thick.

He licks the salt from my mouth and says, 'Mmmm...'

I have to stop him. I need to think about this new...development. It's not good news. 'I'm hungry.'

'Mmmm.'

'Seriously hungry.'

'The color of your hair... Your body... You looked like a sea goddess or a mermaid coming out of the water. In this wretched world you are...perfect.'

His voice is like rich, dark golden syrup. It coats my skin. He kisses my ear and glides his lips along the lobe. The action is like being on a familiar road. I've traveled it before. Many times. Some part of me even knows where this road leads to. I empty my being of thought and surrender myself to desire. It ripples like a forest fire through me, swift and unstoppable. I press my body against his ever-hard bulge in his trousers.

'Would you like that balls deep inside that pretty pink pussy of yours, Miss Black?' he purrs like a dragon seducing a fairy tale princess.

'Yes, I would, Mr. Rose. Very much indeed.'

His hands go around my back and unclasp my bra.

My breasts spill out into the glorious sunshine. Instinctively I straighten my spine so they show themselves to their best advantage. 'What about the men?' I whisper.

'Gone.' My bra lands on the sand.

'Gone where?' Not that I care, but I couldn't think of anything more mysterious or alluring to say.

'To the other side of the island. There is a lagoon there and they've gone to catch bone fish.'

My nipples strain hard against the smooth, hot skin of his torso. I fist a shaking hand in his hair and pull his head down to my aching nipples. He doesn't resist. His mouth on my taut nipple is heady heaven. Heat rushes from his mouth into my body and I feel myself go up in flames. Suddenly the steady sound of the waves disappears and spots dim my vision. I feel dizzy. My knees buckle.

'What's the matter?' he asks, his voice suddenly changed.

Shocked, I sag against him.

'Heatstroke,' he says, and putting his hands under my knees carries me to the house.

'I think I'm fine now,' I say weakly, but to be honest I do feel quite strange. He takes me into the white house and puts me on a long couch under a lazily whirling fan. He goes away and comes back bearing a young green coconut with the top sawn off and a straw in it. I take a few sips and start to feel better.

He crouches next to me, an expression on his face I have never seen. 'How do you feel?'

'Like I could bite your ass.'

He smiles, but that anxious expression remains in his eyes.

'Do you want to rest for a bit?'

'I'm fine now,' I say and it's true—I am.

'Are you sure?'

I put my hand out and erase the frown on his face. This is a side of Jaron I did not expect to see. 'Yes, I'm sure.'

He sighs with relief.

'I'm very hungry, though.'

'OK, lunch will be ready in five minutes.' He kisses me lightly on my forehead and pushes upwards. I watch him walk toward what must be the kitchen. I hear the sound of the fridge opening and look around myself. The house is airy and light. The windows are many and are all open. The furniture is mostly painted wood. Funky and totally cool. Long, transparent green curtains flutter at the windows.

I look at it all and wonder what I would have made of it a couple of hours ago. Sometimes life can be clearly divided into before this happened and after this happened. Important things—before my mother died, after I got cancer, after my son was born. For me it will be after I realized for sure that I was in love with Jaron. The air between us seems to have changed.

Now I have a secret. I am in love with a man who is a total stranger to me and who openly confesses to having a girlfriend. But the relationship is so odd that it even almost seems like a lie. And yet it can't be. Both claim they are in a relationship. Some part of me mourns the loss of my carefree attitude. Another part of me is determined that I will not spoil my time on this paradise island. I am so confused I decide not to think for the next two days.

'What's for lunch?' I ask.

He pops his head around the corner. 'Goat curry, fava beans and rice.'

'What? No fucking way am I eating a goat.'

He grins. 'Just kidding. Mango salad and cold chicken.'

I stand up cautiously. The wooden floor feels cool and smooth under my bare feet. And I feel totally normal so I walk to the kitchen.

'Who made the food?'

'Herbert's wife, Gwen. He's the guy with the dreadlocks.'

With my palms on either side of me I heave myself up on the counter beside the coffee machine. I dangle my legs. 'Hmm.'

He looks at me. 'Jesus, Billie. You're the only woman I know who would haul yourself onto my kitchen counter as if you were a construction worker. Any other woman would have given it a bit more sex appeal.'

I give my chest a little shimmy and watch his eyes change.

'You're going to end up on the end of my cock if you carry on with that much longer.' His gaze blazes with lust and my pulse starts up.

I feign panic. 'I'll have to scream rape.'

'Go ahead and scream,' he advises calmly, taking a step toward me.

I feel his big, hot hands grab my breasts and squeeze them. My nipples harden on his palms. Very deliberately he pinches them. A shuddering gasp escapes me. His eyes sparkle as his mouth comes down on my parted lips in a hot, open-mouthed kiss that makes me groan. His lips are demanding and possessive. I am reminded of the way the dog holds his bitch down in a submissive pose before he mounts her.

He increases the pressure on my nipples. I moan and wriggle my hips restlessly. He breaks the kiss and using his teeth, yes, his teeth, cuts my damp knickers clean off at one side. He pulls them off, chucks them behind him and runs his fingers along the slit full of slick, hot moisture. His fingers stop just before they reach the swollen bud and his eyes travel upward and meet mine.

A slow smile touches his lips.

He circles the bud and I throw my head back so far I am looking at the ceiling. The ceiling is sky blue. I close my eyes with arms and legs splayed open, my hips grinding and rocking against his hand. The pleasure builds.

And builds. I suck in my breath and then he stops. Just simply stops what he is doing.

I open my eyes and look at him half irritated, half in disbelief.

He has taken a step back and is watching me.

'Why did you stop?'

'I thought you wanted lunch.'

'Oh come on. I can't eat like this.'

'Anticipation, Billie. Anticipation.'

'If you don't, I'll sort myself out,' I threaten and put my hand between my legs.

'Don't.' He knocks my hand away. 'It won't hurt you to wait.'

'Why should I?'

'Because it will be even better later.'

I take my hand away.

'Now come and eat.'

'Come here,' I say.

He comes closer. I reach out my leg and put my bare foot between his legs. He is as hard as a stone.

'See. This is harder for me than it is for you,' he says.

'You're driving me crazy.'

'I want to have lunch with you while you are naked.'

He puts his hands around my waist, lifts me off the counter, and puts me on the ground.

'Go on outside and I'll bring the food,' he says and slaps my plump rump playfully.

My legs feel a bit wobbly, but they still work and with a sultry upward glance at him, I turn away and head toward the door that leads to the garden, purposely and exaggeratedly swaying my hips. He grabs my hand and pulls me back toward him. I crash into him, my breasts squashing on his hard muscles.

'Anticipation, anticipation,' I say innocently.

A slow smile spreads across his lips. 'You're on.'

I've never been naked outdoors before and it is both liberating and odd.

We sit on pretty wooden chairs that have been painted with orange flowers on a blue and green background. Someone has spread a tablecloth on the table and set it with colorful plates, utensils, blue glasses, a pitcher of iced water, and a vase of drooping flowers. He holds out the plate of chicken. I spear a thigh and put it on my plate and help myself to the mango salad as he heaps his plate with chicken.

Jaron winks at me and picking up a chicken leg eats it with relish.

I cut a small piece of chicken. It has been smothered in some kind of blackish-brown seasoning, and I feel pretty sure I will hate it. Jaron chews lustily. I bring the morsel to my mouth and pass it between my lips. To my great surprise it is delicious. I must have been hungrier than I thought. I glance at Jaron and catch him looking at my breasts. When he notices that I am watching him watching me he reaches out a hand and rubs his palm against my nipple.

I know he is trying to distract and entice me so I pretend to be unmoved by the provocation and carry on eating my salad. He swallows a mouthful of chicken and then suddenly leans sideways and taking my nipple in his mouth sucks it hard.

I smile tightly. Right. Two can play at this game.

I drop my fork and instead of simply reaching down to retrieve it I stand and bend from the waist so my butt is pushed out toward him and between the crack of my thighs swollen swirls of tantalizingly pink flesh are peeping out at him. I twist and look at him. He is staring quite hungrily at my glistening sex.

'Sorry,' I say sweetly.

He swallows the food in his mouth.

I go to sit down and somehow manage to trip and land in his lap. His cock is so hard it sticks into me.

'Oops,' I say and bounce slightly. His eyes fly to my naked breasts. These fake breasts are great. They bounce very well. I get up, making sure my nipples just graze the side of his mouth before I slide into the chair. Picking up a piece of mango I put it into my mouth, then lick and suck my fingers slowly. I swivel my eyes in his direction. He is properly riveted.

'Would you like some mango?' I ask, knowing he can't very well say no. That would be tantamount to admitting defeat.

He nods.

I take a mango chunk in my fingers and standing up bend forward so my breasts are hanging like low-lying, ripe fruit. I put the slice into his unresisting mouth. He chews slowly and thoughtfully, his eyes flicking from my eyes to my thighs and back to my breasts. I straighten, rest my hip on the table and open my legs slightly. I am like an animal on heat, which come to think about it, I am. I want to lick his toenails.

'Do you know the sea air is having a strange effect on me? I... I...feel wild. I'm actually in a mood to take something really big and hard in my mouth and...suck it. What a shame we have to wait. The thing is,' I add languidly, 'I might not feel like this later.' I lean back slightly on the table so that I am almost stretched out on it.

His eyes leave mine and flick to the raw invitation between my legs. I see that he is badly affected, but I also see his fists sitting on the table. Determined as fuck not to let me win.

Well, I'm not giving in either.

Slowly I slither—and when I say slither, I really mean slither: a snake couldn't have done better—upwards. His eyes are like popsicles on sticks. I sigh elaborately as my nipples trail over the tabletop. Eventually coming upright, I walk to the chair. But this is not the walk of any ordinary mortal. This is the 'I see you shaking that ass' walk à la Billie. I'm giving it all I got.

When I get to the chair I swivel it onto one leg. His head tilts. I've got him. I know I've got him. I put the chair back between my legs and slide my slit along it. I sneak a sly look, filled with lust, at him.

He is staring at me. His mouth is parted.

Now for the pièce de résistance. The chair has two little balls at either end of its back. Slowly, slowly I lower myself on one ball. It is hard and smooth and terribly, terribly taboo.

'Oh,' I gasp and turn to look at him with the ball of the chair inside me.

With a deep growl he stands, sweeps away all the food to the ground, because he is *that* dominant, falls on me, and fucking *devours* me. I stare at the leaves of the Causarina tree as I scream, 'Oh yeahhhhhh.' Did I ever tell you that this guy sucks pussy better than any lesbian? I did? Well, it's worth repeating. He's that good. My muscles start clenching.

'Don't stop,' I command, and fuck him, he instantly does the opposite. He takes his mouth off me. I open my mouth to swear at him, and it becomes a shocked gasp as I am bodily picked up as if I am some life-sized doll and spread on the table, face down, legs splayed open. Before I know it, a big, hard, sun-kissed cock slams into me. The force shoots me forward.

The man's a fucking animal.

He grabs me by the hips and pulling me back, keeps a firm grip on me while he fucks the living hell out of me. Suddenly he stops. Picks me up again, his man-toy, lays me on my ass, spins me around and pushes me back on the table with my head hanging over the side.

'Did I hear you say you were in the mood to suck something very big and very hard?' he asks very close to my ear.

Before I can answer, his cock, covered in my juices, has been pushed into my mouth and right down into my throat. I don't hesitate. I suck for England. It's only fair. But after a while I lie back, close my eyes and allow him to fuck my mouth. He starts thrusting strongly. All I can do is smell the man smell of his pubic hair and taste the saltiness of his skin.

He comes in hot, jerking spurts. Without taking his semi-hard cock out of my mouth, he casually leans over my body and clamps his mouth on my clit and works it until I break apart. It's a good climax. It smells of the sea. He pulls out of my mouth, helps me sit up, and stands between my legs. He runs his fingers playfully in my wet folds and looks regretfully at the chicken pieces strewn on the ground.

'See what you made me do.'

'You started it.'

'Yes, but I'm very, very hungry now,' he says plaintively.

'I make a mean cheese sandwich.'

'I really wanted Gwen's chicken,' he says sadly, and inserts a long finger inside me.

The finger is distracting but I keep my head. 'You've got a cheese sandwich. Take it or leave it.'

'You're a hard woman, Billie.'

We break apart at the sound of the men coming back with the fish they have caught. It is funny to watch him hopping into his trousers. I sit on the table, reeking of sex and as naked as the day I was born, and laugh.

By the time he comes back into the house with the fish, I am wearing one of his T-shirts and have already cobbled together his sandwich. He puts the fish—the men have gutted and cleaned them—in the sink and goes to sit at the table.

I slap the plate with the sandwich in front of him.

He opens the richly buttered bread and looks at the filling: thick slices of cheese and tomato in layers. He raises his eyes up to me and grins. 'Dude food?'

I grin back. 'Exactly.'

He picks it up and takes a big bite. 'The milled pepper is a nice touch.'

'Thank you,' I say graciously.

I sit next to him and watch him wolf it down and feel almost protective of him. Woe betide anybody who tries to hurt him. It's an odd thought.

Fifteen

That afternoon we take it easy. Jaron shows me around the little villa. There is a room with a mirrored wall and exercise equipment, a spare bedroom, two bathrooms, a kitchen, a storeroom, a dining room, a porch and our room, the master bedroom. It is dominated by a huge cream bed. A mosquito net hangs over it like a cloud.

'Very romantic,' I say.

'Mossies will eat you alive without the net. They are terrible, the only drawback to this place. Make sure you spray on a lot of bug repellent before the sun sets.

'OK.'

We swim and go snorkeling. The water is super clear because it has been a calm day and he points out all kinds of fantastically colored fish and marine life.

When evening comes we stand on the beach and watch the sun setting. The sky is almost purple. It is unforgettably beautiful. Jaron twines his hands into mine.

'What happens after sundown?' I ask.

'Nudity,' he says with a smile.

I laugh. 'How much nudity?'

'Lots.'

Jaron barbecues the fish that the men caught and we eat them. They are succulent and wonderful the way food never is when you are not truly hungry. After the meal I have a shower. The water is brackish. Then we sit on the beach covered in bug repellent drinking rum and talking.

'Listen,' I say, suddenly catching what seems to me to be the sound of music.

'It's a party on the mainland,' he replies.

'Wow, the sound travels that far?'

'Sometimes when the air is very still you can even hear a dog bark.'

'Really?'

'You want to go?' he asks.

'To the party?'

'Yeah.'

'Of course I want to go to a Bahamian party,' I say enthusiastically.

'OK,' he agrees.

'We're going to crash their party?'

He smiles. 'See you need to get into island mentality. This is not England where you need to let people know that you are going to come around. Here people just drop in. More or less everyone on the mainland knows me. I'm usually invited.'

'Great. I *love* parties.'

'Come on then. Let's go.'

I change into an apple green top with spaghetti straps, tight red pants and the only pair of shoes I have left, now that my other pair is lying at the bottom of the ocean. But the gold sandals actually look glitzy and partyish. I layer on the mascara and slap on the gloss and I am ready.

'Looking good, Billie,' I tell my reflection.

'You look amazing,' Jaron says from our bedroom doorway.

I turn around and look at him. He is wearing all black again. In the dim light, he looks mysterious and positively unreachable. I walk up to him and touch him. A thrill of something potent but secret runs up my arm. The desire for him doesn't abate but just becomes stronger and stronger.

'I don't know why I did that.'

He grins. 'I don't know either, but I like it.' He runs his index finger down my cheek reflectively.

Suddenly I feel nervous. I smile weakly. 'You're staring.'

'So are you.'

I pretend to grin. 'I can't stop. What's your excuse?'

'Same,' he says very quietly, with no trace of humor in his voice.

He bends his head and claims my mouth and the kiss—I don't even know if I can describe it as a kiss—is a mess of all things: it's soft and yet hard, caring and yet fierce, liberating and yet possessive.

For a while I resist the conflicting demands of the kiss and then I give in, and I find myself in a slow dance. But it is not us who are dancing. It is our souls, entwined, swirling, merging like liquid. It is so beautiful and profound it hurts. When he breaks away, I touch my mouth and stare at him in awe. I feel almost drunk. My pulse is racing like mad.

'What the hell was that?' I whisper. My voice sounds tiny and scared.

'I was carving my name into your heart.'

I look at him, the hottest man in every room. The man who already has a girlfriend. 'What the fuck did you do that for?'

'Because you're the most beautiful fucking thing I have ever seen. And I was claiming you.'

I look at him. I'm being stitched up. I'm walking into a massive elephant trap. 'How can you claim me when you've already got a girlfriend?' I hate the whiny sound of my voice.

'Sometimes things are not as they seem.'

Something small and fragile blooms in my heart. I want to be coolly sarcastic. Laugh and say something richly comic. But I can't. I have to be true to the moment when our souls mingled.

'What do you mean?' I whisper.

'One day, Billie. One day soon I'll tell you. Now: are we going to this party or not?'

I take a deep breath and smile, intoxicated the way no drug or amount of alcohol has ever made me feel. 'We are.'

We take the small, shallow boat. It has a huge headlight on it that lights the way through a long, deep water channel that belonged to an old salt company. It shows the way into the bay. I have never been on a boat at night and it is a-fucking-mazing. The water gleams dark and mysterious. The cool wind blows in my hair and face and the occasional sea spray that showers us is exhilarating. I love the sensation of my hand trailing in the water, which is still warm from the day's sun. I urge Jaron to go fast and faster. The speed is addictive and the feeling of flying headlong into the darkness is crazy.

When we get to the mainland Jaron secures the boat and helps me out. My hair is a mess. He runs his fingers through it and smoothes it down. 'I love the feel of your hair when you don't use half a can of hairspray on it,' he says.

'Well, make the most of it. I love my hairspray. Just forgot to bring it.'

We walk along the beach. He holds my hand. It feels right. On our right, dark vegetation rises up like an impenetrable shadow. The sand is so soft it gets into my sandals so I take them off and carry them in my hands. The sand is cool on my feet. There is no moon. The only light is from the torch Jaron carries. Little transparent crabs scurry along the sand in front of us. There is the ever present sound of the insects in the trees and the faint sound of music.

In the distance we see the lights of the party. It is being held on the beach outside a wooden house. There are lanterns lit around it and a bonfire is going. Lana Del Ray's *Summertime Sadness* starts playing on the loudspeakers and I feel a thrill of excitement run up my spine.

'Come on,' I urge excitedly, tugging Jaron's hand. 'I love this song. We have to dance to it.'

He looks down at me amused, but he nods, and like a pair of kids we run toward the party. There are many people there and most of them either call out to Jaron or wave at him. I drag Jaron to the middle of the throng of people dancing. This is one of my favorite songs. If I close my eyes I can actually see it like waves in the air. I find a gap in the crush and gyrate to the beat.

Jaron stands a foot away from my body and watches me. There is passion and possession in his eyes. Then I swagger closer to him and sinuously sliding my hands onto his shoulders rub my body all over his. I want him all over me and I am saying it in no uncertain terms. He grins, his eyes at half-mast, and moves his hips to match mine. It's casual. And it's damn sexy.

I pull his body so close I feel his erection. We gaze into each other's eyes. The music changes and I don't really notice. He ushers me around a corner and pushes me up against the wall of the house with his lips. The music is so loud it is rattling the wall of the house that I am pressed against.

'Right now all I want to do is suck your wet cunt loudly and hungrily,' he says. The thought is so fucking erotic I soak my knickers through there and then.

'I didn't know men loved eating pussy that much.'

'I don't know about anyone else, but I can't fucking get enough of yours. I dream of eating your pussy,' he says, and claims my mouth in a hard kiss that takes my breath away.

'Hey, lover,' someone calls from behind us.

Jaron takes his time about releasing my lips. 'Later,' he promises, his hot breath mingling with mine. Jaron turns around and I see a man, his startling white teeth flashing in the darkness.

'Look at you,' the man says in a really cool accent. 'You brought a sweetheart.'

'This is Noel,' Jaron introduces and then turning to Noel with a wry smile says, 'And the sweetheart is Billie.'

'You finally went and fished yourself a girl, huh?'

Jaron rubs his chin thoughtfully. 'Yeah, but she's a bit of a handful.'

I punch Jaron on the arm, hard.

Jaron pretends to wince and rub his arm and Noel laughs. 'It's island love.'

A woman comes to join us and Noel introduces her as his wife. She has the most amazingly beautiful brown skin, the exact color I would have chosen to have if I had been given a choice in the matter, and she is wearing big hoop earrings with beads in them, which I covet. She has an Afro hairstyle. She grins at me and Jaron.

'I love your hair,' I tell her. 'I used to have an Afro when I was in school.'

'Was it the fashion then?'

'Nope. I just liked it. I still do. I might yet have one,' I say and feel Jaron's eyes on me.

'A green Afro might be pushing it even for you,' he says with a chuckle.

'It's teal, not green. And I'll do as I like with my hair,' I say haughtily.

'Did you enjoy the chicken?' asks Gwen quickly.

'Very much. It was delicious,' Jaron replies smoothly. 'But there wasn't enough for me. Billie ate most of it.'

Noel laughs hard, his eyes twinkling, and I wonder if he knows what really happened to the chicken.

'I will cook some more for you tomorrow,' says Gwen.

'Would you?' asks Jaron beseechingly. He sounds so different with Gwen that I turn to stare at him. There is no mask, no barriers. Just boyish enthusiasm.

'Noel will bring it,' she says, nodding firmly.

'Thank you,' both Jaron and I speak in unison. It's a strange thing to speak in unison with someone. It has never happened to me before. We smile at each other.

'You two are already drunk on love, but come and have some rum anyway,' invites Noel with a chuckle. The statement is casual but explosive to me. I dare not look at Jaron to see his expression. I turn toward Noel eagerly.

Rum, I must say, is a drink I enjoy very much and it flows very freely that night. I make friends with everybody. The mainlanders must be the friendliest people on earth. They laugh uproariously at my jokes and teach me all kinds of really cool phrases. Bust up means badly drunk; you can intensify anything by adding the word dead in front: dead cold, dead ugly. To sip, sip is to gossip, Jack means friend, leg short means you have arrived too late for something, to be without money is to be break. I consume more and more rum and it is all great fun. Everything is funny as hell and I am the life of the party.

A man in an open blue shirt carrying a guitar comes and sits opposite us. Jaron introduces him as Terrance. Someone switches off the music. The air fills with the sound of the waves and human voices. Terrance smiles broadly and starts strumming his guitar. Soon the place becomes silent but for his guitar, the crackling of the fire and the incessant waves. It is very peaceful. I turn to look at Jaron. His blond hair shines in the firelight. Terrance starts singing. It is a strange song. I must be very drunk because I am unable to catch all the words but some stick in my head as if they have been nailed in.

Understand the truth of the flowers.
Become the lord of the flowers...people...cattle.

*Become   the   lord   of   the
flowers...people...cattle.*
Understand this truth.
Fire is the in-dweller of the water.
Understand the truth.
Understand your in-dweller.

I am too drunk to make any sense of it. I frown up at Jaron. 'What's the song about?'

'It is about us, people. We who live our lives like cattle.'

For a moment I stare at him. Is he serious? 'What do you mean?'

'It is a cry of the soul, the fire inside the water, to wake up.'

'Wake up?'

'Most of us are sleepwalking through life. He is daring you to explore your inner world.'

'Yeah,' I say, looking at Jaron with new eyes. There could be something more to this man than meets the eye. Something deep and profound. Terrance has finished his song and starts singing Bob Marley's, *No Woman No Cry*. Now this I can understand. A few songs later, Terrance packs up his guitar and music from the loudspeaker fills the air again.

Time to dance again. I get up and go for it.

When *Feeling Hot, Hot, Hot* comes up on the loudspeaker, the crowd actually parts for my solo. Fueled on alcohol and Jaron's hungry eyes I give it all I've got.

I am still dancing when Jaron picks me up bodily and says, 'Time to go home, Dancing Queen.'

'Awww... Don't be so dead boring,' I slur drunkenly and bring my glass of delicious drink—Noel's famous gin and coconut water cocktail—to my lips. He takes the glass out of my hand so fast I am left staring at the empty space where the glass had been.

'Say goodbye to everyone,' he says firmly.

Some of the men jokingly tell Jaron not to spoil the party by taking me away.

'See? They don't want me to go,' I tell Jaron.

'Sorry, guys, but it's my bedtime,' Jaron says good-naturedly.

I stand on my tiptoes and whisper in Jaron's ear, 'I ain't going to bed until you show me all kindsa shit.'

'Right you are, beautiful,' Jaron says coolly, catching me as I stumble.

Noel grins at me. I say my bleary goodbyes and let Jaron lead me to the boat. I have to admit the return journey on the boat is not nearly half as much fun as the journey there. I lie at the bottom of the boat feeling quite sick. Instead of urging him to go faster I yell at him to slow down. 'Oh God! I'm going to throw up.'

The man is pitiless. 'Just hang your head over the side and throw up,' he shouts. Fortunately, it never gets to that and thankfully the ride is fairly short. The engine is cut. As I loll about at the bottom of the boat in a state of inebriated self-pity, Jaron comes to me. He stands over me with his legs spread wide to steady himself in the rocking vessel. I squint up at him.

'Give me a hand then,' I groan.

His answer is to heave me up like a sack of potatoes onto his shoulder.

'Whoa,' I cry.

He walks me up the path and opening the front door takes me directly into the bedroom. The cool air from the air con makes my sticky skin tingle. It feels wonderful. He puts me on the bed and I look up at him. His hair is messy with the wind and a whole shock of it has fallen on his forehead.

I raise my hand and pinch his rough cheek. 'You are so cute,' I tell him. 'I could take you to bed.' I spoil it by then yawning widely.

'You're totally wasted, aren't you?'

'No, I'm not,' I insist, but my words are slurring so badly they are almost indecipherable.

'Bed for you, I think.'

I snake my arms around his neck before he can straighten. 'No, no, no. I want to fuck...you.' I smile feeling inordinately proud of the way I left that pause between fuck and you.

He raises a disbelieving eyebrow.

I let go of his neck and start trying to wriggle out of my pants, but it's difficult to accomplish in my condition. I look up at him. He is standing over me, stone cold sober, just watching me.

'Help me then,' I demand.

He holds both the ends of my trouser legs and tugs hard just once, and my trousers slide out from under me like water.

'Smooth,' I tell him in an impressed voice. 'Now my top.'

He makes even shorter work of that. I slide a finger into my knickers and look up at him with flirtatious eyes.

'Last bit,' I say invitingly.

He slides them down my legs and off my feet. His eyes inspect me. I like that! I open my thighs wide and say, 'Come and get it, big boy.'

Sixteen

I wake up in a very uncomfortable position. In fact, it is surprising that I managed to sleep in such a position at all: on my back totally trapped under Jaron. One of Jaron's legs, bent at the knee, is under my butt and the other is lying on top of my stomach. One of his arms is under my neck and the other is thrown across my body, the hand possessively covering my breast, and his head is buried in the crook of my neck.

For a few seconds I don't move. Then I slowly start to extricate myself, mainly by bringing one of my arms up to remove the hand that is stuck on my breast. The moment my hand wraps around his wrist, his grip tightens and a small protesting sound comes from under my chin.

'You owe me,' a sleepy voice says.

I swivel my eyes down to the top of the dirty blond head. It looks very silky, like the head of a boy. 'Owe you what?'

He lifts his head and looks at me. His eyes are green, but calling them green would be like calling Da Vinci's *Mona Lisa* a painting. His eyes are like the carpet of moss that grows only on certain stones. It is fresh and bright and only found in secret gardens where humans don't bring their business.

'Don't you remember?' he says slowly. Right before my eyes, the colors of his gaze change. They seem more liquid and blue-green like the tropical ocean seen from the sky. He can't decide if I am serious.

I shake my head. The action properly dislodges the headache that was hovering at the edges of my consciousness. Damn hangover.

He gets his arm from under my neck, lifts himself on his elbow and looks at me with surprise.

'What is the last thing you remember?'

I dig through my mind. 'I know I had a great time and that I absolutely love Bahamian people. I remember coming back on the boat. Oops, and nearly being sick overboard.'

'Mmmm...'

'Then I think we came back and went to bed, right?'

'No, you promised me a lay, opened your legs wide and passed out.'

'I did?'

'I want to claim my lay now.'

'Well, you can't. I have a splitting headache,' I say, frowning and exaggerating my malaise.

'I'll be so gentle you won't even notice I'm inside you.'

'Yeah, right.'

'I'll start and if you notice that I'm fucking you, just tell me and I'll stop.'

'Do you even know how big your dick is?'

'Yeah, but I'm working hard to ruin you. After me, baby, all other men are going to be like shoving pencils into your vagina.'

In spite of myself I have to giggle. 'Can't you take no for an answer even once?'

'No.'

'Ah,' I exclaim and suddenly find the entire lot of Jaron Fucking Rose lying on top of me.

'Fine,' I say, determined that I will be such a wet blanket that he will not enjoy it either.

He grins, and sprinting off me energetically and extremely lightly starts by targeting the one place he has found on my body that makes it impossible for me to resist. My big toe.

'Ahhhhh...'

He takes my big toe out of his mouth. 'Can you feel me yet?'

'No.'

He puts his mouth back on my toe and sucks gently. Oh! Heaven. His large hands start traveling along my calves. I must really like him, I've shaved my legs. A fact that he has noticed and seems to appreciate. One by one he does all the toes. I wriggle them in his mouth and he swirls his tongue around them. It makes my body arch with pleasure. He puts the right foot down and takes the big toe of the other foot into his mouth and gives that a good ole suck too. By this time I can feel the heat of watching him suck my toes in my groin. He starts kissing the inside of the soles of my feet.

'Ah fuck... Jaron.'

'Did you feel that?'

'No.'

His mouth moves along the inside of my calves and sucks at the backs of my knees. My thighs start trembling. He moves up until he is so close to my throbbing core I feel his breath on me when he obsequiously tells me, 'If I'm making your headache worse, just tell me.'

'All is still good,' I croak, my sex aching for release.

He licks at the slit and then opens the lips with his fingers and even widens the passage with his fingers, but he doesn't hang around very long. Maybe he knows I won't last this morning. That I'm about to explode any moment now. He lifts himself to his knees. Raised in that position his hair catches a beam of morning light coming in through a gap in the curtains and glows like spun gold. I watch in awe as this blond god slides me down the bed and lifts my hips to the level of his.

And then he very deliberately, solemnly, and gloriously drives the full length of his thick, hard sex deep into me. Stretched wide and filled to the brim I gasp and weaken all over. The overwhelming impression is that of being impaled, possessed, and taken. With one arm he supports my hips while with the other he plays with my clit. The sensation of his slow and deliberate fucking and the relentless caressing circles he makes are hypnotic and irresistible.

My body drenches with pleasure. I feel myself float closer and closer to the edge and my hips start snapping against his so his thrusts become cruel too. That pushes me over the edge and my body arches so rigidly it lifts his body with mine and somewhere in my moment of exploding pleasure I hear his groan of release. Hot fluids fill me as I lay gasping.

Still held up by his hips and dick I moan softly. He watches me with a satisfied look on his face and then he withdraws out of me and puts me down. He sits between my parted legs and spreads apart my knees so wide that my hips rise up and off the bed, buttocks split open and my exposed sex feels as if it is protruding and hanging down. It is a humiliating position but his hands on my knees are powerful and will bear no objection. And this position also reveals my sex to be a craving thing. It wants him. It wants everything he wants to give it. It flutters open and closed like a desperately hungry mouth. He gently massages me between my legs, smearing the juices leaking out of me into my lips and stroking my sticky clit.

'Not again,' I object, but weakly. I am greedy for it and because that orgasm really did take a lot out of me I feel lethargic and exhausted.

'Again,' he says very firmly and between my legs, my sex throbs helplessly at the brutal dominance in his voice. I shiver, trying to restrain its greedy throbbing.

'What's the matter?' he whispers, his hands expertly working the moist flesh.

 146

I flush bright red. I cannot admit to it but I cannot help being violently turned on by the feeling of being overpowered. There is a certain amount of shame to being overpowered but at that moment the path of acceptance seems more hospitable. I gasp as the pleasure between my legs mounts and mounts. His fierce fingers strike the wet, throbbing flesh.

'Oooooo...' I sob as the waves come. The sobs are a delicious release for the warm pain. Moisture trickles out of me and runs down the crack of my buttocks. He smiles and using that slick wetness inserts his finger straight into my ass.

Seventeen

I get out of the shower and feel slightly fresher but my head is still throbbing. I slip on my bikini bottoms and go into the kitchen. I know exactly what will cure my hangover. The hair of the dog. Jaron is bent over something at the kitchen table. 'What are you doing?'

'I'm repairing your watch. It was running late.'

'You can repair watches?'

'Sure. I'm very handy with anything that is full of tiny springs or precision machined to close tolerances. When I was young I spent hours completely dismantling watches and locks and putting them back together.'

'Great.'

I open the cupboard and reach for the vodka bottle. A large hand covered in golden hairs curls around my wrist. I jump. I didn't hear him come up.

'Don't,' he says softly.

'What?'

'You drink too much, Billie.'

'What?' I repeat in disbelief.

'You heard me.'

'Who the fuck do you think you are?'

'How old are you now?'

'Fucking none of your business.'

'Let's say you're twenty-two or three. You'll be an alcoholic by the time you are thirty-three.'

'Fuck you,' I say angrily, but some part of my brain is recoiling in fear as I lash out. I yank my hand out of his grip and deliberately take the bottle and pour myself a huge measure. I gulp it all down very quickly while he watches me expressionlessly.

I put the glass down with a 'take that and put it where the sun don't shine' thump, but in fact, I have drunk it too fast and I feel downright queasy.

He stares at me. 'What's the matter?'

I turn around and run to the bathroom where I am violently sick in the toilet.

When I put my head up Jaron is holding a wet towel. I don't look at him. I take the towel from him silently and wipe my face. He goes out and I brush my teeth before I follow him.

'I've made coffee,' he says, holding out a mug.

'I'm sorry I was so rude,' I say.

'It doesn't change anything. You drink too much.'

I put my head down. I know he is right. It feels like fun, but I've seen enough alcoholics on the council estate to know where I am heading.

'You don't need it, Billie.'

'Sometimes I do.'

'Sometimes we all do. But you even drink in the morning. It's not cool, Billie.'

I take a sip of coffee and make a face. I hate coffee.

'Can I have some orange juice please?'

He pours me a glass and hands it to me with two painkiller tablets. I take the pills and drink the whole thing down. I realize how awfully dehydrated I must have been.

'How about we agree that you'll drink when you need to and when you're out having fun, but no more vodka bottles in your bedside cabinet.'

I glower at him and every fiber in my body rejects being told what to do. That is my MO. No one, and absolutely no one in the past has told me what to do. I do what I want. Period. I don't buy the 'do it for your own good bullshit' from anybody. And to be honest, if it had been anyone else other than him I would already have decimated them to an insecure blob of jelly by now. And yet I can't with him. Some secret part of me is craving for him to take control, to care enough to make me do it.

I nod. 'OK.'

He grins. 'You made that too easy. I was prepared for a huge fight.'

'You don't know when to stop, do you?'

He raises both hands as if to ward me off in mock alarm.

And it is impossible not to laugh. He takes me into his arms. His face is so tender it makes me feel quite strange. Our relationship seems to have suddenly become really serious.

For some reason that makes me fearful. 'I want something back from you in return.'

He stiffens imperceptibly. 'What?'

'Let me drive your car?'

I feel it then, that great big wave of relief that washes over him. I wonder what he thought I was going to ask of him.

'I'm making breakfast,' I say.

'You are?' His eyebrows are in his hairline. A bit irritating, that.

'Mmmm...'

'I'd better keep it simple then. Just eggs.'

I go to the shelf, take an egg out of the carton and throw it directly at him.

He moves so fast even I am startled. He catches it neatly between his loosely cupped hands, looks at me, and smiles wryly. 'I really wanted cooked eggs.'

I smile. I am determined to know more of the man. I know nothing about him. I walk to the cupboard I saw him take a pan from yesterday. I take out a pan, put it on the stove and look around me.

'Top cupboard to your right,' he says.

I open it and take out the plastic bottle of oil. I pour the oil into the pan, wait for a minute and then smack the egg on the edge of the pan and pour it in. Great! It has kept its shape. I crack another egg and it too keeps its shape. Jaron puts two slices of bread into the toaster. He brings jam out of the fridge and puts it on the kitchen table with a bowl beside it. I really want to turn the eggs over but I dare not. I turn to look at him and he says, 'Sunny side up is fine with me.'

I breathe a sigh of relief and turn down the fire. When the toast is ready he puts it on a plate and taking a metal spatula from a drawer comes over to me. I take the metal spatula and carefully slide his eggs onto his plate. I am inordinately pleased with myself when the eggs go onto the plate unbroken. My first ever lot of cooked eggs and they turn out so great. Yay!

I look at him with a victorious grin and he is staring at me.

'What?'

'Thank you,' he says softly, and I just know he is not talking about the eggs, but I am suddenly too shy to ask what. We sit at the table and I watch him shake salt and pepper on the eggs.

'How long have you had this place?' I ask filling my bowl with jam.

'Five years. It's a queen's ninety-nine year lease,' he says, buttering his toast.

'Do you have brothers or sisters?'

'No, I'm an only child,' he says casually, but suddenly I feel the care and caution that come into his face.

'Are your parents still around?'

'Yes.' His voice becomes even more distant.

'Where do they live?'

'In Australia.'

I feel a movement in the corner of my eye, turn to the window and see that a stork has landed in the garden. It is very beautiful. For a moment it stands very still and then it drops its head and gracefully pecks under its wing.

'There is a stork in the garden,' I say quietly.

'Yeah, they drop occasionally.'

I could have turned around then, but I don't. I am not so foolish as to turn around and expose myself to his devastating weapons. To allow him to wrap his sensual spell over me. 'Why did you go to Monte Carlo?'

I wait for him to answer and he doesn't so I turn to face him.

'Why all the questions, Billie?'

'No real reason. It just occurred to me that I know nothing about you.'

'In time you'll know everything there is to know.'

Suddenly I feel very naked and exposed sitting in my bikini bottoms. Jaron's T-shirt is draped over a kitchen chair. I take it and slip it over my head. Now we are both hiding from each other.

Because of high winds the water is cloudy so we do not go snorkeling. Instead we have a sandcastle building contest. Jaron's is bigger but mine is definitely better. Afterward he buries me in the sand. He takes photos of me and when it is his turn I give him large conical breasts and that looks really funny. We laugh a lot. He breaks out of the sand and chases me into the water.

We swim in the nude, our bodies slipping eel-like against each other in the silky water. We start kissing in the water and end up on the beach where the waves still touch our feet and Jaron's tongue is everywhere all at once. We make long, languorous love on the hot sand, the sun beating down on us, and the ticklish waves sometimes reaching up to our hips.

'Sticking my cock inside you is like sticking it in a wall socket,' he murmurs in my arms, sleepy with the exertions of pleasure.

I bury my face in the hair that smells of sun and sea and me. The reality of love has surpassed anything I could have imagined. I remember when Lana told me she was in love, and I had arrogantly claimed I never wanted to be under another person's control or power. And now my words have come back to haunt me. My life seemed so empty before he came. I can't even imagine life without him.

At nearly two in the afternoon we go to the mainland for lunch. Jaron wears sunglasses, which make him look like a really cool movie star. He takes me to a shack, painted bright green with purple doors and yellow window shutters. The sign is in faded blue. It's funky. And I like it a lot. Plenty of beers are cooling in a huge metal drum full of ice. A man called Ernie whom I met at last night's party owns the place.

He makes an especially super-strong rum punch and puts it in front of me. 'On the house,' he says with a broad grin.

Jaron shrugs.

'Oh dear, looks like my reputation has preceded me,' I say, taking a sip. It is delicious, but I remember what I have promised Jaron, and I don't drink it as fast as I normally would.

We order barbecued chicken and sweetcorn local style. Jaron has chutney and one tiny drop of their scarily hot Scorpion Pepper Sauce, which he cautiously spreads on his chicken. It's H-O-T-T-T hot stuff. Two drops, I am told, would make the food inedible! Even the label carries a warning to use it with discretion and not recommended for children.

I heap my plate with fried plantain (yummy) and local avocados. Just when I think I am nearly done, Ernie comes out with hot dogs and burgers. We go into the tiny town where Jaron takes me to an old bell tower church. We climb to the top and can see for miles around.

Afterward we go into a little convenience store in the town. It is a rustic, sleepy place where there are no schedules to keep and everything runs on slow time. Jaron buys some pasta for our dinner. We go back to Ernie's to drink one of his cocktails and watch the fading light dancing over the sea and the sand. Ah, the sand. So soft, so white, so pristine.

Eighteen

That night there is no moon. The islanders call it the dark night. A perfect time to catch land crabs. We go to the other side of the island where there are mangrove trees to hunt for some.

To catch them, Jaron lies on his side on the sand and sticks his whole arm up to his shoulder down into a hole in the ground while I shine the torchlight into the hole. It looks really dodgy to me, putting one's arm into random holes in the ground, but Jaron tells me that even though the crabs are very skittish and sensitive they are blinded by the glare of the torch. They will stop in their tracks and only move again when the light is no longer on them.

'What if it's the home of a snake or something?' I ask worriedly.

'Snakes don't live in crab holes,' he says totally undeterred by my reasoning.

'You have done this before, haven't you?'

'All the time. There's an art to it.'

The first hole is empty. He reaches all the way into the other end of the second tunnel we find and comes up with his first catch. I scream. The crab's body is the size of a fucking softball and its legs are about twelve inches long. And it also has a very large fighting claw. The claw alone is bigger than my hand.

'Want to try?' he offers.

'No fucking way. I need both my hands.' I shudder at the thought.

He laughs.

'How many do you plan to catch?'

'Maybe six.'

'They are so big. Why do we need so many?'

'I want to give them to Noel. Gwen makes a mean crab rice.'

'Right. Will she kill them?'

'Yup, after she has purged them. She keeps them in a cage and feeds them water and cornmeal until all the poisonous leaves and disgusting things they have eaten have come out of their system and then they are ready for eating.'

I nod and point the flashlight at another hole in the ground.

When we have six in our sack we return to the house.

'Want to join me in the shower?' he asks.

'No.'

'Sure?'

'Yeah. I'll just sit here and wait for you.' He goes in to wash and I sit watching the movements the crabs make in their sack. They seem pitiful, and doomed, crawling helplessly over each other. In the end I can bear it no longer—I take them to the end of the beach and upend the bag. They crawl out, seemingly dazed for a few seconds, but they recover quickly and crawl off in different directions. I sit on the beach and stare at the waves. It's very peaceful.

Jaron comes to sit beside me.

'What happened to my crabs?'

'I let them loose.'

'I see.'

'I guess I am one of those proper hypocrites. Give me an indistinguishable packet of crab flesh in the shape of a dumpling in a Chinese restaurant and I'll chow it down, but show me a live crab and I become Mother Theresa.'

'I always secretly fancied Mother Theresa.'

'Even her tree roots feet?'

'Maybe not those.'

I smile. There is something tight about his mouth. He doesn't want us to carry on with the conversation I started. I hate prying. I've always minded my own business and never been nosy or even wanted to know what other people were doing. Even while they were telling me their business I was bored and often told them to quit it. And now for the first time in my life I want to know about someone else's business and he doesn't want to share it. Serves me right, I suppose.

'Are you hiding something from me, Jaron?'

He winces. 'Maybe. But it's not important.'

'OK.'

He hugs me. Hard. And suddenly I know: it is important. His secret is important.

'Has it got something to do with Ebony?'

Silence.

'Maybe.' His voice is very quiet.

'Can't you tell me?'

'I will. But not yet. I need to trust you.' My stomach descends in my body. I know with every fiber in my body that he is not sneaky, but I don't like the sound of any of this at all.

'OK.'

'Want to try the Jacuzzi? I switched it on.'

I feel heavy-hearted, but you know what? I'm not about to lose my shit. I'm just here for the sex. Everything else is whatever! For some strange goddamn reason tears are gathering at the backs of my eyes. Why?

'Let's go,' I say in a high, bright voice and stand. A little voice says, what's the matter, Billie? You jealous? No, I fucking am not. I'm not devastated. I'm not gutted. I'm just pissed off. And pissed off sex I can do. Until his dick rots off.

So we go to the Jacuzzi and the sex is wild and angry and, in spite of the way I feel, explosively good. By the time we get out Jaron is looking at me funny.

'Billie?'

'Fuck you.'

I stomp to the kitchen and pour myself a massive glass of rum. I drink it down like milk. And the breath that exists in my mouth could burn a rat to ash.

He stands at the doorway.

'What's eating you?'

'Nothing's *eating* me.' Asshole. And then something comes to rest upon my heart. It's not his fault. It's me. I thought I was liberated—that I could do the sex thing without wanting to get possessive and jealous and crazy. But the truth is I can't. I want to call him mine. I fucking hate that Ebony is in the picture. 'Just leave me alone.'

'Is it the crabs?'

'Go fuck yourself. Stop irritating me. I don't want to talk to you.'

'Well, what do you know? I want to talk to you.'

I start pouring another glass. He comes and takes the glass from my hand. I glare at him.

'You don't need this.'

'How dare you!' I literally scream at him.

'I dare because I care.'

Something! Something vibrant and alive, something stronger than the best chemical high happens in my head. It shines. It illuminates. On the mainland a man is fucking a prostitute, a dog is foraging in the bins, a taxi swerves to avoid a bus, a man buys a woman a drink. I look into Jaron's green, green eyes. They are festering with splendor.

You'll regret this, Billie Black.

Yeah? Maybe. Maybe he is duping me, but from where I am standing his eyes are transparent windows into his soul. Just reams and reams of honesty. He grabs my arm. Brings me to his hard body. Strange how I can't even imagine a soft body now.

'I want to be inside you all the time,' he says.

'And I want you inside me all the time,' I confess. The wound closes up, stops bleeding. Ah, that is how you heal the damn thing.

He kisses me. I come up gasping for air. I should leave it alone. But I can't. I'm not made like that. I have to know the truth even if it hurts me.

'Who is Ebony?'

'Are you jealous?'

'No, I'm fucking not.'

'Then it doesn't matter.'

I scowl at him. 'I don't want to go out with someone who has a girlfriend.'

'Why?'

'What do you mean why? Do you know of any other woman who would put up with that shit?'

'But you're not like other women. You're unconventional. That's what first attracted me to you.'

'All right, I'm jealous,' I shout. 'Blindingly jealous. Jealous enough to rip your fucking eyes out. Now who the hell is she to you?'

'She's not my girlfriend. I work with her.'

'Not selling real estate, you don't.'

He smiles, but it is a sad smile. 'No flies on you.'

'Erin told me that they have a really cool saying here—don't let your mouth carry you where your foot can't bring you back from.

Why do you introduce her as your girlfriend, Jaron?'

'She makes for good cover.'

I swallow hard. I have wanted to know for a long time now. And now I will. 'Why do you need cover?'

'I'm a jewel thief, Billie.'

Nineteen

I blink. 'You're fucking what?'

'I'm a jewel thief,' he says slowly and clearly.

'What the hell does that mean?' I demand.

'It means I target and steal the rarest, most precious stones on earth.'

'So if you rob a safe and there is cash in there you won't take that as well?'

He shrugs. 'I would but it would not have been the cash that drew me there in the first place.'

I shake my head wonderingly. 'So you're a criminal? A common criminal.'

'That's one way of looking at it,' he says totally unfazed.

'What other way is there?'

He shrugs. 'It's a semi-conscious form of social revenge.'

'Social revenge? Semi-conscious?' What the hell is he on about? I am so stunned it kind of all goes over my head.

'Hasn't it ever occurred to you that the distribution of wealth in society is wrong to begin with? The outrageously rich are outrageously rich only because they have employed a variety of legal and illegal ways to steal from the rest of us. All I'm doing is righting the balance.'

The breath comes out of me in a rush. 'Are you serious?'

'Yes, perfectly. I *am* a predator, but only to the ultra ritzy, rich vein of society. The ones that surpass me at thievery. Coming down to wine and dine at magnificent tables laden with silverware and fine food they sometimes find I have set a place for myself.'

'So it's not like, why work when I can steal?' I ask sarcastically.

He spreads his hands out. 'There is an element of that.'

'This is a profession where you can't keep the pot boiling too long. Sooner or later you will get caught. You do know that, don't you?'

He smiles. 'I know that. Master criminals are the stuff of fiction. They don't exist in real life. But in the end, it is just the one life. What's more important? How many breaths you take? Or how many moments take your breath away? My conscience is clear. I will die a peaceful man.'

'It's wrong. You're stealing from people.'

'Believe me, I choose my targets very carefully. The reason I have never been caught is I always leave a souvenir, a little tape of them misbehaving, behind. Catch me and the souvenir becomes public. These people are liars and cheats and pedophiles for whom the loss of a piece of jewelry is equivalent to you dropping a glove in the park. Sometimes they stage their own break-ins many months or even years later and collect the insurance anyway.'

I frown. 'Shouldn't you be giving this information to the police, especially about the pedophiles?'

He laughs bitterly. 'When I made the first tape I was still young. It shocked and horrified me and I thought the world should know what this world leader was up to. I sent copies of the disgusting tape anonymously to the police and the media. I waited for days, and guess what? Nothing happened. Everything went on as before. We live in a sado-masochistic culture, Billie. It is a curious paradox of our society that no section of it is more addicted to sadistic behavior than those entrusted to prevent it: the judge, the police commissioner, the cop, the prosecutor, the politician, the industry leader, the media mogul... They cover for each other.'

'So you are like some sort of Robin Hood?'

'That's one aspect. There is another more compelling aspect. I do it because danger is a compulsion for me. Even as a child I was always what the psychologist would term chronically bored. I needed more stimulation than others. I was glue sniffing, smoking, drinking, fucking anything in a skirt, taking drugs, fighting, indulging in random acts of vandalism, and motorbike racing just to chase away the boredom. The first time I stole I was sixteen. There was a very large house at the end of my street where a widow had lived alone. When she died her children began fighting over the will and it had been empty for some years. I broke into it one evening.

'It was as if I had entered Miss Havisham's house in *Great Expectations*. All dust, drawn blinds, silver candelabras and antimacassars. But I can never forget the thrill of that first plunder. My mouth was dry, my heart was racing: the rush of larceny is like an orgasm, only better, so much better. I grabbed a bottle of brandy, a crystal ornament, and rushed up the stairs. The first door I opened was a bedroom. I opened a drawer and rifled through a woman's silken underwear and felt almost dizzy with excitement. The sexual stimulation combined with plunder was indescribable, a feeling that was to stay with me all my life.'

'And that's it? You just became a thief at sixteen?'

'Stealing is like any other profession. There is an art to it. It's not all shinning up drainpipes and creeping into gutters. You've got to master the craft and use your brains. I learned very quickly that I had to fit in perfectly with my victims' backgrounds— Mayfair, Belgravia, the Hotel de Paris in Monte Carlo, 41st to 43rd Street in New York, an English stately home, the Sydney Opera House, Ascot Races... You are never a suspect. You blend in with the wealthy, the famous and the greedy. Finding the right victim is paramount. The anticipation of the heist is like an imminent orgasm. The frisson of excitement before, during and immediately after a coup is indescribable.'

'And you made all your money by stealing?'

'No, I made a great deal of it by investing in the right properties. Mostly in London.'

A thought occurs to me. 'So you stole the blue diamonds you gave me?'

'No, I bought those.'

'Why buy when you can just steal?' I ask suspiciously.

'There is a protocol attached to selling stolen jewelry. Pieces have to be broken down to their parts so they are unrecognizable. In fact, offloading rare gems will soon become impossible once they are laser printed with their own signature markers.'

'How does Ebony come into the picture?'

'I almost always work alone, but occasionally she will undertake some small part.'

'So she's not your girlfriend?'

'For a while she was. For a very short while. It was a mistake. Pleasure and business don't mix... You're the first person I've ever told this to. I know it must be very hard for you to understand.'

'I once stole a rocking horse from Mamas & Papas,' I say quietly.

He frowns. 'Why?'

'At that time I couldn't afford to buy it and I wanted it for my godson. I didn't feel bad doing it—I knew that big companies like that have an allowance for pilferage. It didn't have a security tag on it so I just picked it up and walked out with it.'

'Ah, the most important trick of larceny. Bottle! The more blatant you are the more lawful it looks. Do it in broad daylight and carry a card that identifies you as a Fire Prevention Officer.'

'So what happens now?'

'I don't know. Meeting you has confused me.'

'Confused you how?'

'I haven't worked it out yet. Let's just take it one step at a time, OK?'

'OK,' I say quietly, but joy is bubbling up inside me like a little fountain of water that has found its way from deep underground into the sunshine.

Twenty

We leave the island and arrive back in England late in the afternoon. It is raining—big fat drops of cold rain. Nothing could be more different from the place we have left behind. I feel a little sad and a little frightened. We did not have sex last night. We simply cuddled and fell asleep in each other's arms. The truth is I wanted to have sex. I wanted it to be as though nothing had changed. I was afraid that something had changed. And I wanted back the carefree, wild way we had been.

Even after that first night something inside my body changed. Like he flicked a switch and everything I thought I was, everything I wanted, suddenly disappeared. And all that is left now is an aching hunger... Impossible to satisfy without him.

When we reach his house I realize that I am far more exhausted than I thought. Perhaps I am even a little depressed. I know now that I can't just ride into the sunset with him. There are problems—big problems, maybe unsolvable ones. He undresses me, slips one of his T-shirts over my head and puts me to bed. Not in the white room, but in his bed in his bedroom. His room is very large and full of light that comes from the sky. I look around tiredly. It is a sumptuous room. Chocolate and cream and beautiful old paintings. I guess it's a man's room.

He puts me into bed and gently kisses my forehead.

'Go to sleep,' he tells me, the way an adult would instruct a child, the way I tell Sorab.

I close my eyes and almost immediately fall asleep.

I wake up alone. I don't call out. I simply get out of bed and go looking for him. There is no one upstairs so I go down the magnificent marble steps. I wonder if a time will ever come when I will not be impressed by their beauty. The banister is cold and smooth under my hand. I hear a whirling sound, like the blades of a fan going very fast. I go toward the sound. It is coming from the room with all the gym equipment.

I open the door and Jaron is in the middle of the room. He is dressed only in a pair of faded, loose, knee-length shorts. He is skipping but he is going so fast that the rope is a blur. It is the rope that is making the sound. He is moving from foot to foot. The movements he makes are very graceful and light. You would never believe it of a man his size. I close the door and lean against it watching him. He stops and looks at my reflection in the mirrored wall.

'What?' he asks.

'You don't want to know,' I say watching his back muscles gleam with a sheen of sweat.

He turns around and faces me. 'Actually, I really do.'

'I was thinking about licking the salt off your back.'

He throws the skipping rope on the ground.

'That is usually a punishment I reserve for naughty girls. Have you been naughty recently?'

'Yes, I was very naughty this morning.'

I lean forward and lick his nipple. It's salty. I snare it between my teeth. 'You smell like a bearskin rug,' I mumble, and increase the pressure on the nub. Not even a flinch out of him.

'You've never smelt a bearskin rug, have you?' His eyes are mocking.

I let go of the nipple. There are teeth marks on it. 'OK, you smell like what I think a bearskin rug smells like. Makes me want to get naked and lie on top of you.' He reaches out for me and I evade his hand.

'Aaa,' I say warningly and move around him.

I stand behind him and with great dedication I abandon myself to the job of licking the sheen of sweat off his back. He shudders and turns to look at us in the mirror. I swivel my eyes to look too. The picture we make is distilled sex. The slow licking looks obscene and that is perhaps why it is such a turn-on.

I feel myself getting wet. We watch ourselves avidly. Both of us mesmerized by what our bodies are doing. I slip my hand into his loose-fitting shorts and feel for the elastic of his smalls. With both hands I yank them both down his narrow hips. Wow! Instantly his erect member stands proud. It is always me who is nude while he is dressed. For the first time it is the other way around. It's kinda hot.

'Play with yourself,' I tell him.

He palms his mighty schlong and starts to stroke himself, all the while watching me. I feel rather pleased with myself. Maybe I miss being in control, making the other person submit to me. I stop licking and walk to the front of him. We look at each other. His jaw is clenched hard, but the expression in his eyes is maddeningly arrogant. And it occurs to me that he's not doing what I want. I'm doing what he wants. Suddenly he moves—the movement is so sudden and quick it feels like an explosion of sheer male power and aggression.

To my shock I am now facing the mirror and he has grabbed me by the crack of my ass, his fingers digging into my pussy. Impaled thus he lifts me until I am barely on my tiptoes and walks me in that position toward the mirror. A foot and a half away from our reflection he stops.

'Hey, that's not fair,' I squeal.

Using the hand buried between my legs he lifts me higher so I am clean off the ground and in such a precarious position that I am forced to place the soles of my feet and my palms on the mirror and straight off I see what his intention has been all along. Evil bastard. Now he's driving the train.

In the mirror my long T-shirt is bunched up around my hips, the soles of my feet are filthy, and between my spread thighs my sex has opened up like a flower, but also I see his large, manly fingers crudely buried inside my glistening hole. Underneath my pussy his erect cock bounces.

It could be the most vulgar and most horny thing I've seen in my life. Exposed and vulnerable and totally helpless in his firm hold. It looks so wrong and yet so badass good. Oh, hell yes.

He stands there scrutinizing my dripping bits. The lips of my vulva rolled back in anticipation.

'Dirty bitch.'

'Yes, quite,' I say.

With a long finger he strokes the flowering part of my clit. 'Play with yourself,' he says smoothly. His smile is triumphant.

The power struggle between us makes my skin tingle, but he is also my sexual soulmate. Between us there are no inhibitions. Nothing is out of bounds. It also causes a maddening ache between my legs. My breath races, but I am so incensed by the way he has tricked me I think about refusing.

'You want to come, don't you?' he whispers in my ear.

I stare at Mr. Alpha stubbornly.

'Do it,' he orders.

I use my finger and begin to play with my clit.

'Look at me while you do it.' His voice is domineering.

I look at him. At the pleasure he takes in taming me as I carry on playing with myself. I don't take my eyes off him even as I succumb to the orgasm coming for me. It turns me inside out. I rock helplessly around his hand. When it is over I close my eyes, breathe gently and lean my head back. He kisses my neck.

'Milk time for pussy,' he says, and lowering me to the floor, tilts my pelvis upward, and fucks my pussy into oblivion. Well, I don't just stand there. I match him in his thrusts, impaling myself over and over on the hard rod.

'Jesus, you're one wild fucking beast,' he says.

'Yeah, feed the fucking cat,' I pant aggressively, and lose myself in a haze of lust and heat and friction until he comes, spurting hot semen deep into me. He stills, heaving, his face buried in the side of my neck, and I squeeze his cock as hard as I can. It twitches inside me and he raises his eyes to me. His hands blanket me. One cups my breast. I turn my face toward his and we kiss.

Slow, tender, careful, and I feel myself float on a warm wave and dissolve into his mouth. His tongue and lips make love to my mouth while he crawls under my skin and into my heart. There is no other way to put it.

Twenty-one

Ebony rings my bell in the afternoon. I open the door and stand aside.

She enters wordlessly. I lead the way to the living room.

'Can I get you a drink? Vodka? Goat's milk?'

She shakes her head. She is wearing something that looks like a super-sheer, giant condom. To give her her dues, she has the figure for it.

'Have a seat.'

She eases herself onto my sofa.

I walk to the sofa opposite her and sit down. 'Well, what brings you here, Ebony?'

She smiles at me coolly, but I can see that she is seething. 'You've been to the island?'

'Yes,' I say shortly.

She smiles tightly. 'He's so predictable. Takes all his conquests there.'

A hot bubble of pain starts in my bowels. The thought: he has taken her there. He takes all his women there.

'What do you want?'

She smiles. 'Did he catch land crabs for you?'

I want to slap her hard, so hard I leave marks, but I swallow hard and keep my cool. 'Is that what you came here for? To ask about my holiday?'

That puts her back up. 'Of course not. But he is very good at catching land crabs, isn't he? He has the long arms of a gorilla. It is easy for him.'

'True, he has beautifully long arms.'

'So you had a good time?'

By now I am barely hanging onto my temper and yet I know she is here for a reason and that she has secrets I want. 'Yes, I had a *very* good time. Was there something you wanted, Ebony?'

'In fact there is. I wanted to tell you that while you are enjoying Jaron's large cock, don't forget that you're just a temporary diversion. One of many. You can't even begin to guess how many. The man's a slut. But I'll always be in his life. We have something special. It transcends sex.'

'Ah, that'll be why he took me and not you to the island then.'

Her eyes glitter with hatred. Jaron has no idea, but this woman is crazy in love with him. 'You don't know anything about him,' she snarls.

'What is it I should know?'

She smiles a nasty smile. 'Ask him what he does for a living. I think you will be rather surprised by the answer.' With that she stands up and sails toward the door. I stand up and go after her.

'I know what he does for a living,' I tell her.

She laughs. 'Oh yeah?' she taunts. You see, she has one final, ominous parting shot. 'Then ask him why he chose you.'

I close the door after her. My mind is blank. I light a cigarette. My hands are shaking so much I stare at them in surprise. I go onto the balcony and watch her walk down the street toward an illegally parked bright yellow Mercedes. It is one of the ones I have always liked. Jaunty. The SL400.

A parking attendant is busily writing a ticket for it. Even from here I can see the ingrained expression of sanctimonious and self-righteous indignation on his long face. He has nearly finished writing his ticket. I exhale smoke from my mouth. My attention flicks away from the attendant to Ebony. She is strolling toward her car. There is not an ounce of distress or worry in her stride. I would have been running toward my car, waving my hands wildly, and cursing loud enough to wake the dead. Jewel thieves probably don't have to worry about pissy parking fines.

The parking attendant has already written his ticket, torn it off, put it into its yellow and black plastic case, and is in the process of pasting it on her windscreen when Ebony leans all her hot curves against the bonnet of the car. He turns and goes rather rigid. Then he fidgets and I can almost imagine him blinking and gulping. Who knows what Ebony says to him, but he looks around aggressively, as if demanding, 'What? What the fuck is a mere man supposed to do in such a situation?'

She says something to him and he actually preens. I've never seen a man preen. She tears the ticket from the windscreen and holds it out to him. It flops in her hand. The wind picks up and it waves half-heartedly. Like some sort of white flag. For a moment longer he hesitates. Then he looks around again and fidgets. Suddenly the ticket is back in his hand. She blows a kiss, gets into her car and waves at him, then revs her engine loudly before roaring off.

And I stare at the sky and wonder what the hell I am going to do with my situation. It feels as if I have been left holding someone else's parking ticket.

After a while I decide. I am not going to play into her hands. If she wants me to ask him then that is the wrong thing to do. Let him tell me when he is ready.

When you're twisting in the wind, don't spit.

Twenty-two

Jaron Rose

They chased him through brambles,
They chased him through the fields,
They'd chased him forever,
But the fox would not yield.
              —'End of the Game' by Sting
https://www.youtube.com/watch?v=wqxn5POGoGI

I walk the night clad in black. Unknown. Unseen. Unchallenged. A shadow among shadows. Rooftops to me are a home away from home. Like smoke I drift along them, slip into the most well-guarded keyholes, work around ultrasonic motion detectors, and drop a leg onto a smooth, rain-slicked ledge, so narrow it is more an architectural flourish than a shelf broad enough to house the dimensions of a human foot.

Let me tell you, when all you have are your hands and back flat against the wall and your shoes stick out over the edge of a twenty-one floor fall—one sneeze or one truly malevolent gust of wind and it's all over—it is an indescribable adrenalin high.

This is the thief's world: a life of compulsion, great passion, skill and danger. It is a fantasy world where it is a risk to disturb the grime on a windowpane. A glamorous world of priceless objects and a space where seconds can be more precious than hours or days in the ordinary world. It is an intoxicating, overwhelming, and addictive business. But it is not for the faint-hearted. It's all about challenge.

Sweat always breaks out on my brow when I pull on my black gloves, and fear, that old friend of mine, takes a stroll across my stage. At that moment I always smile, a grim smile of welcome. Only when you welcome the fear can you master it. Fear is useful—it alerts the senses, but only the intellect allows control.

After this initial surge of fear I become ice cold.

Normal people will find the long shadows caused by the low-level, non-invasive red service lights that virtually all galleries in the world employ murky and oppressive. Not me. I revel in them. They turn soaring vaulted ceilings into low, black voids of mystery. The arid tang of de-ionized air expelled by coal-filter dehumidifiers in museums: it's perfume to me. And those security cameras mounted high on their walls that frighten you into not touching anything, well, let me tell you, they are not real. Real video would be too expensive to run. Most museums rely on containment technology. Take an Italian masterpiece off a wall and the gallery immediately seals itself with you inside it.

When I think of myself I see myself silently weaving my way over a roof, or crouching on my haunches, or balanced on a parapet scanning for sighters on the street. It is what I was born to do. Even as a child I could shimmy up a tree like a koala bear.

But sometimes I think of myself falling seventy feet below onto a line of spiked protective railings. The spikes impale my thighs in two places. I have never forgotten the pain of pulling my flesh off of the unforgiving metal, leaving behind blood, bits of flesh and gore. I wake up sometimes haunted by that fall. In my nightmare the spikes enter my heart. Even so, I wouldn't have it any other way. I'd do it all again.

Even the fall.

You see, real life, the one led by most people, is excruciatingly dull. Too dull for me. I'd rather be a persistent sinner. And I am that.

I didn't tell Billie the whole truth!

I wanted to, but I didn't.

I told her I was a jewel thief and I gave her the impression that I do it for the danger. The high of knowing that this could be the last time and going ahead anyway. That my greatest passion comes from creeping on a roof, making a tunnel in a wall, avoiding the latest in security to get that loot. That is only true up to a point.

I was that. I walked around with an empty rugby bag to fill with spoils, but that was only until that day when, while sorting through a jumble of gems and glitter, ordinary pieces of diamond, out of someone's safe, I realized I had landed a rare and magnificent 40.63 carat, heart-shaped Burmese ruby mounted on a 155 carat diamond necklace.

I held it up in the shine of my heavy-duty torch and a stimulus came from it. It was not sexual like the act of stealing. It was far more potent than that. It was love at first sight. It provided me with more satisfaction than any woman had ever provided.

I was captivated—mesmerized actually. I suddenly understood why people kill for these shiny objects. For me it was like standing on the deck of the sinking *Titanic* and debating if we would not have hit the iceberg if we had gone a little bit slower or steered the ship a little more to the north. The deed was done. The ship was sinking.

The compulsion to steal more of these beautiful stones is incredible, undeniable. The high is unobtainable by any other means. I have tried everything. Kinky sex in strange nightclubs, places where nothing is taboo, but nothing compares to stealing and collecting these beautiful objects.

Why didn't I tell Billie that?

Because telling her that would reveal something else. Something she will not like. My mobile rings. I look at it. It is Ebony calling. Something that involves Ebony. Something unfinished.

Twenty-three

Billie Black

I wake up early that day. Impossible to sleep.
All night long I tossed and turned. Jaron did
not spend the night with me. He said he had
an important thing to do. And when he said it,
I had an awful feeling in my belly. A
premonition.

'What is it that you have to do?' I asked
him.

'It is not dangerous. I just have to help a
friend,' he said.

'I'm afraid,' I said.

'Don't be. It is nothing.'

'Can I come with you?'

'Oh, darling, I wish I could take you, but I
can't.'

So I slept badly, woke up before dawn and
spent my time drawing. But I could not
concentrate and I hated everything I came up
with.

I am surprised when the phone rings. It is
Lana.

'Did I wake you?' she asks me.

'I wasn't in bed,' I tell her. Her voice sounds
strange and strained.

'What is it?' I ask her. I think I know even then that it will affect me. I close my eyes and wait for it. And it comes just the way I feared it would.

'We were burgled last night,' she says.

'What?' My voice is hoarse.

'Don't worry, your sapphire is in the bank. There were only a few pieces in the safe.'

'You were robbed?' My voice is a shocked whisper.

'They bungled it, though, and the police have already caught one of them. A woman.'

I feel, I actually feel the blood drain from my face. 'A woman?'

'Yes, a woman. They have her in the cell and—'

'Lana, what's the woman's name?'

'I have no idea.' She pauses with surprise. 'Why?'

'I just need to know. Can you find out?'

'Of course. I'll call Blake later and ask him.'

'No. Now. I need to know now. Please.'

'Billie, what's going on?'

'I promise I'll tell you everything. Just find out her name first.'

'OK, call you back.'

I end the call and dial Jaron's number. His phone is switched off. My hands are trembling. I clasp them tightly together. I unclasp my hands and cover my face with them. There must be some other explanation. I stare at the phone. The truth is I am unable to do anything else but stare at it. My mind is blank with shock. I want to tuck into a tight ball and simply sleep. When the phone rings I jump like a startled cat.

'Billie,' Lana says, and just by that one word I already know. 'It's Ebony.'

I close my eyes.

'What's going on, Billie? She is accusing Jaron of being the ringleader.'

A small, involuntary sound escapes my lips. In my head, I see Ebony taunting me. 'Ask him why he chose you? Ask him why he is in your life?' Of course, it all makes perfect sense now. When he met me at the exhibition he was casing Lana Barrington's jewelry. I remember that night with incredible clarity. That's what they were doing. Now I understood why he was so curious about Lana in the beginning.

And I was the idiot in the middle who led him to the crown jewels. I took him to Blake's house. I made it easy. I try to remember, did he pause to look at the alarm by the door? Of course, he had always been curious about Lana. My breaths come in uneven gasps. Sorrow like I have never experienced, never imagined existed, hits me in the gut. I'm going to fucking cry.

'I've got to go. I'll call you later,' I choke out.

'Billie, I'm coming over,' Lana says.

'All right, come over.'

The line goes dead and I feel my eyes begin to fill with unshed tears. He used me. It was all a lie. All of it.

Suddenly I feel faint. Helplessness surges into me. I want to howl with anguish and horror, but I can barely whisper. I hold back the angry tears, but my throat starts squeezing and my eyes simmer painfully. Shit. I'm gonna cry. I do my best to blink them away but one or two start sliding down my cheeks. I see the expression in his eyes change. Pity? Fuck him. I'm not having anyone feel sorry for me. I force myself to sit down and show that I am calm. But my heart is as cold as a stone in winter.

'Oh my God, Oh my God,' I repeat as the tears flow down my cheeks.

I have never been in such a situation before. Always it is Lana who is in trouble or who requires a shoulder to cry on. I am the strong one. When she comes through the door I am shocked to see the change in her. Like a different person. She wraps me within her slim arms and holds me for a long time. And for all that time I simply stand and absorb the love that pours out of her.

My chin trembles and I try very, very hard to get myself back in control. And in the end I do. And she must have felt it. With her hand still around me, she guides me to the couch. I sink down. It is a relief to sit. To have her take charge.

The first thing she says surprises me.

'I don't care if it was him, I'm not pressing charges.'

I stare at her dumb-founded.

'Blake is going to talk to Ebony and get some facts. Do you know where Jaron is now?'

I shake my head. I feel such a fool. I've been so stupid. So blind.

'Don't worry, Blake's people will find him.'

I nod and then I look her in the eye. 'I knew he was a jewel thief. And I didn't care. He was stealing from the super rich. He was like a Robin Hood.' My voice breaks on a sob. Listen to me. I sound like a total idiot. Robin Hood. He used me to steal from my friend. 'I'm sorry. I'm sorry he stole from you. I'm sorry I brought him to your house.'

'Oh, Bill! Please don't be sorry. I would have given you those jewels if I thought you wanted them. They are not important to me. You are.' She pauses for a moment. 'And Jaron. Jaron is important to me too.'

'What do you mean? He lied to me and abused your trust and friendship.'

She shrugs. 'I liked him from the first moment I met him, but I always had reservations about Ebony. So I'm not going to believe the worst of him until he has had a chance to explain.'

I look at her, shocked that she wouldn't give up on Jaron. At her refusal to judge him. Her phone rings and she takes it out of her bag and looks at it. 'Let me take this call. It's Blake.'

'Hi, darling,' she says into the phone and then starts listening. For some minutes she listens. Then she rings off and turns to me.

'This is what Ebony is claiming. Most of the heists are executed by Jaron alone, and once or twice she has been involved, but this time they connected with some low-level Mafia and it went wrong.'

'Yes, he did tell me that he mostly works alone.'

She frowns. 'After all these years why would he contact the Mafia this time around then?'

'I don't know.'

'Something doesn't feel right.'

I feel too exhausted and miserable and angry to answer. The shock is dissipating and in its place is a burning ball of anger. I don't feel forgiving or loving or like I don't want to judge him. Jaron Fucking Rose is a bastard!

Twenty-four

I feel overwhelmed by a dizzying sense of loneliness. I don't fucking need him. I lie on the bed holding my vibrator. I lean my head back on my pillows, close my eyes and part my legs. I switch it on. And I think of him. I think of him when he kneels down in front of me and puts his mouth between my parted legs and drinks from my sex, and the desire roars through my body like a storm. The way dark blood rushes to my clit and everything becomes a flooding liquid. Just sucking and heat and hunger and furious fucking. I open my eyes and throw the vibrator across the bed.

I have a key to his home.

I call for a minicab and go to his house. I stand outside and look around me. A woman is walking her beautifully coiffured poodle. She gives me a condescending look. As if I'm in the wrong neighborhood. At another time I would have said something to her. But my mind is blank. I go up the steps and put the key in the door and then I realize I cannot go in. I will set the alarms off. I left the code at home.

I ring the bell. No one answers. I turn away and walk toward the Tube station and feel even more unhappy than I had felt before I came and saw the deserted house. Maybe I'll get the code and come back, but I know I won't. I feel drained.

I take the Tube home in a blank daze. I sink heavily into a seat and look up at the map. Only five stops and then I become so sad I can hardly move when it is my stop. I force my stiff body up and stumble out of the doors. At home I go and sit on the bed. For a while I am so stunned I sit and stare blankly into space. It doesn't matter what he has done, I want him so bad I want to punch him for being so stupid, for using me, for cheating. Eventually I work myself up to a grand rage.

Absolutely livid, my mind falls upon the idea of getting drunk, getting so totally wasted that nothing matters anymore. I think of the vodka bottle that is in the kitchen cupboard. A full bottle. I haven't touched it since I made that promise to Jaron at the island. I haven't needed it. I need it now. I feel like a caged animal. Today I need that feeling of calm spreading in my belly. Like warm milk. I will sleep then.

I go into the kitchen and yank open the cupboard door where the vodka is kept. With a furious grunt I yank it from the shelf and something flat and small wrapped up in a piece of paper falls to the ground. My hair stands on end. For a few seconds I cannot do anything but stare at it. I put the bottle on the counter and run my suddenly sweaty palms down my trousers. Then I pick up the package curiously. The paper is a note and it guards a key. My throat feels dry. I unscrew the vodka bottle and take a swig. My head feels as if it is spinning. I wipe my mouth with the back of my hand and look again at the note.

```
Go to the other place.
Beware of being followed.
       112986316
It's all yours.  JR
```

For many seconds I do nothing. My mind ticks furiously. He knew what I would do, but he also hid this note. The first thing I do is let my eyes carefully scan the room. Sorab's cereal box is out farther than I usually leave it. I walk out into the living room. The leg of the sofa is not sitting in its old indent on the carpet. I run to my workroom and my drawings are in totally different places from where I left them.

I go back to the kitchen and study the note again. Then I exchange my bright red top and blue pants for a gray hoodie and black jeans. I learn the numbers by heart. I make a pocket in the pad of one of my bras and slip the key into it before wearing it. I take the battery out of my mobile phone before stuffing it with two large cloth bags into a small handbag.

Then I slip out of my apartment and walk to the Tube station. There I surreptitiously look around me. A man—he is young and thin— looks away as I meet his eyes. I won't look in that direction again. The train comes and I board it. Five stops later I get out and start walking to the opposite platform. I sit on the bench and wait. A train comes but I don't get on it. I look around casually and notice the man standing at the far end of the platform. When the next train comes I get into it. As the doors are closing I lunge out. The train whooshes away.

I look around me. There is no one but me on the platform. I run up the stairs and make for the Central line. There are only two Asian guys and a woman with a pram on the platform. An elderly woman appears. She looks at me with hostility. I have never seen her in my life. I am being paranoid.

The train is due to arrive in one minute. It arrives. I get on it and change again at Tottenham Road. I sit alone in the carriage and watch the train tear through the darkness of the tunnel. I get off at Goodge Street station. Here the amount of people thronging around me makes me feel safe. I get out of the station and take a taxi. I don't go directly to the apartment.

I go to the coffee shop down the road and order a glass of orange juice. I sit with my drink and settle my nerves before going to the toilet and removing the key from the padding of my bra. I slip it into my pocket and casually walk to the building. It is on a quiet street. Most probably why he got it in the first place. I look around me and there is no one about. I read the names against the bells. So Myra lives in Flat 3. I give her direct neighbors a miss and ring bell number thirteen. No one answers. There is no one at Flat 14 either. I hit gold with Flat 15.

'Hey,' I say making my voice sound as young and apologetic as possible. 'This is Myra from Flat 3. Could you please let me in? I've left my key at home.'

There is a rude grunt and the door buzzes open.

I push it and enter. The lobby smells dank. I have a flashback of coming here with Jaron that first night. I was so high and excited I did not notice the smell or the dankness of it. I am too hyped to wait for the lift. I run up the stairs and hear my own footsteps reverberating loudly in the empty stairwell. To the third floor. I put the key in Jaron's door and enter.

Inside I lean against the door panting for a minute. My heart is pounding so hard I can barely hear myself think. All the curtains are drawn shut and it is dim. The flat is exactly the same as it had been that night. Spartan. Clean. Unwelcoming. In fact it has that sepulchral, crypt-like aura about it. I put my handbag on the hardwood floor, hurry to the bedroom and switch on a light. It is cold in the bedroom. I look around me quickly. The bed is made. I have an image of it unmade with both of us naked and clawing at each other. I don't dwell on the image. It is not lost. I can still have it back.

It is almost a cliché but I run to the wardrobe and tap on it. Well, what do you know? It is almost too easy. I feel a surge of excitement. I tap in different places and find that the whole fucking thing comes back hollow.

I sit back on my heels and stare at it. I yank all the clothes from the clothes rail and throw them on the ground. I start looking around the sides. The edges are all smooth and clean. It is too neat and well built. I know what I am looking for and I am closer than I think. In the end I find it. A little button just behind the door. I push it down and grin.

The panel slides back, so smoothly and silently that my eyebrows rise with admiration. The admiration turns to awe as the panel reveals what lays behind it. An oblong vault door made of solid steel. The rivets are so huge they are like those you see in bank heist movies. An electronic lock blinks at me. There appears to be a fingerprint scanner but Jaron must have switched it off and only one light is glowing red. Shaking with nerves and excitement I key in the numbers in my head and the light becomes green. Grasping the massive lever I heave the heavy door toward me. It swings open slowly.

A room, an actual room yawns at me.

My skin tingles with anticipation as I take a step toward the darkness. I have the feeling that entering into it is akin to crossing an imaginary threshold into another world.

Jaron's world. I enter it without a second of hesitation. I feel the sides of the door and locate the light switches. The spotlights that come on blind me. I blink and then my eyes widen with wonder.

Wow!

I look around, my mouth open. The room is no bigger than about six by ten feet, but its walls are lined with glass cases and in them are the most marvelous, staggeringly beautiful jewels. There is a large armchair a step away from me and I collapse into it. This is where Jaron sits admiring his loot. I bring my feet up and curl up in the comfy seat. There is a small round table next to the chair with a remote.

I press play and the classical music fills the room. I don't rate classical music. I have always thought it is boring music for boring people. I kinda like being tasteless and the lover of the lowest common denominator, but at this moment, this piece of music is perfect. It is fast and precise and full of drama. I imagine Jaron sitting here, with a glass of champagne, simply admiring his beautiful jewels.

By their fruit ye shall know them.

For a long time I sit in the armchair looking at the dazzling pieces of jewelry in wonder. For the first time I understand what he meant when he said jewels are frozen music. The clarity is fierce and all-consuming. I know what I have to do.

I spring out of the chair and going back out into the flat I retrieve my handbag and take out the cloth bags I had stuffed into them. It seems I had always planned to do this. I take the cloth bags back to the secret room. For a moment I stand framed in the doorway. I wish I could take a photograph, but I can't for obvious reasons. Never mind—I will never forget this sight as long as I live. This amazing room that Jaron created. I go to the first showcase. It is not even locked. I press the glass and it springs open silently. I run my finger on the square pink stone. It must be a pink diamond. He has touched this. I take it away from its black velvet stand and hold it in my palm, savoring the weight of it. I hold it up to the light and it sparkles like crazy, scattering little pieces of light on the floor.

I roll them all in toilet paper and bag them all quickly.

In less than an hour the room has been ransacked. It looks strange. I feel a bit sad to think I have dismantled Jaron's life's work. But I switch off the light, close the safe, slide the panel carefully back, put the clothes back into the wardrobe and close it. I switch off the light and, opening the door, leave the flat carrying two plastic shopping bags. I go down the stairs and taking a deep breath exit into the street.

No one pounces on me. Phew.

I walk quickly down the road and disappear into the Tube station. When I emerge it is in Victoria station. I buy a couple of small suitcases and put the bags into them. Then I head on over to left luggage, check the bags in and return to the Underground. On the Tube I put the battery back into my phone. I emerge out of the network in Green Park. I get out of the station and call Lana.

'Hey,' I say. 'I need to talk to you and Blake.'

Twenty five

Blake's private plane drops me off on the mainland. I take a boat out to the island and get the man to drop me off in the sea, swimming distance from the beach.

'You sure?' the boatman says.

'I'm sure,' I tell him and jump into the water.

'Must be island love,' he says, grinning and starting his motor.

I kick off my shoes, pants and top and then I begin to swim. I spot him immediately. He must have heard the engine of the boat.

He is standing alone, a mountain of a man, his hands jammed deep into his trouser pockets, staring out into the sea. He looks so abandoned and so despondent that my heart bleeds for him. This is my man. For better or worse I'm sticking to him.

When my feet touch sand I begin to walk toward him. It is that first morning we arrived. Me coming out of the sea. Him watching and waiting on the beach. I come out of the water and walk up to him, my feet sinking in the soft sand noiselessly. About five feet away I stop walking and we gaze at each other.

Oh God, the sight of him.

In two days he has already picked up the kind of golden tan that I would kill for and there are blond streaks in his hair that I have fantasies about. Something quivers inside me. Damn it, he is just so mind-numbingly handsome it is unfair. Objectively, the guy is more fuckable now than I have ever seen him before. An image of him naked flashes into my mind.

He takes his hands out of his pockets and lets them hang loosely by his sides. I love his hands. Big, manly... Useful. For putting into crab tunnels. For the first time since I have known him he seems tongue-tied.

'Hey,' I greet softly.

'I didn't run away,' he mutters.

I barely catch it over the sound of the waves. He sighs. 'I was working on a plan. You had to know that I chose you over the stones.'

'I know that.'

'And I wasn't part of the team that tried to rob Lana's jewels either.'

'Oh! I *know* that.'

'I was going to steal the pink diamond pendant that Lana wore to the art exhibition, but that was before I knew she was your friend.'

'It's OK, baby. I know you were not trying to hurt me.'

'I love you. You know that, right?'

Tears start slipping quietly down my face. 'That's good because I'm crazy about you.'

He takes two steps toward me. 'I want to marry you.'

I grin through the tears. 'That's real handy. I always wanted to be married on a beach.'

'I'll have to go straight. We might have to pay taxes and stuff.'

'That's OK. I'm quite rich in my own right.'

He looks at me quizzically. 'You returned the jewels, right?'

'Some,' I agree non-commitally.

For a few seconds he looks at me with a mixture of shock and disbelief, and then he grabs me as if he *owns* me and pushes me to the soft sand and falls sprawled and laughing on top of me.

'Tell me,' he growls.

'I gave Blake a few token pieces to return to their rightful owners in exchange for you.'

He looks at me curiously. 'Blake bought that? He's too sharp.'

'Of course he didn't, but I told you there are benefits to being his wife's best friend.'

'Where are the gems now?'

'In left luggage, Victoria Station.'

'You left hundreds of millions worth of jewels in Victoria station?'

'Relax. It's the safest place for them.'

He laughs and runs his fingers along my cheekbone. 'Oh, Billie. You are a girl after my own heart,' he says, and there is such a look of love and tenderness that I feel my insides melt. I look into his eyes, molten gold in the bright sunlight and the reflections of the sand. My face feels hot and there is already a wet throbbing in the soft flesh between my thighs.

'Do you feel like fucking?' I ask, arching my eyebrows.

'Always.'

'Because I'm ready to explode in a very unladylike way.'

He looks at me the way I would look at a very beautiful gerbil. 'I love you, Billie. I've never felt for anyone or anything the way I feel for you.'

He takes my bra off and starts kissing my breasts. 'You know,' he murmurs, 'I think I fell in love with you in that club on the very first night we met.'

'And that's why you didn't call me, huh?'

His gaze is warm. 'I always knew I was going to call you. There is no one in the world like you, Billie Black. But I had problems. I didn't know you were friends with Blake and Lana. And then Ebony became angry and contacted the Mafia and my cover was blown forever. The best way to get caught is to lose control and team up with impulsive psychopaths. I didn't want to do it so she went behind my back.'

'She's in love with you, you know.'

'No she isn't,' he retorts instantly.

'You're such a man. So clueless.'

He frowns.

'She came to see me.'

'A fat lot of good that must have done her.'

'Oi! Whose side are you on?'

'Yours, yours and yours.'

'Keep going.'

'I've actually got to show you something.'

My eyes flick meaningfully to his crotch. 'Take off your trousers then?

Patience, Black. Patience. He sits up and twists away from me, and I see that his entire back is filled with a massive spider tattoo. It is still raw and fresh.

'Oh my god,' I cry.

'Do you like it?'

'I love it,' I scream. 'But why?'

He shrugs. 'I never could before. I was always trying to blend into the background of the titled, the moneyed and the famous. I'm finished with all that now.'

'It's totally boss.'

'Good. Because I did it for you.'

'Does this mean you get to be on top until that spider heals?'

He cocks an eyebrow. 'Let's get one thing straight, Miss Black. You're *always* going to be underneath me. Got that?'

'Loud and clear.'

His grin flashes. 'Now get fucking naked.'

'Make me,' I say.

And he does.

The End

Want More Hot Romances?

Click on the link below to receive news of my latest releases, fabulous giveaways and exclusive content.
http://bit.ly/1oe9WdE

Want To Leave A Review?

No matter how short it may be, it is precious. Please use this link:
http://amzn.to/1ol1v0m

Want To Stay In Touch?

☺ Come and say hello here:
https://www.facebook.com/georgia.lec arre

**Interested to know more about Blake and Lana Barrington?
Read about them in The Billionaire Banker Series.**

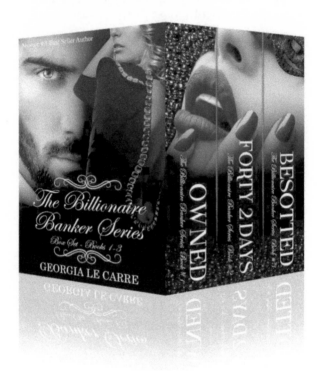

Links:

Amazon.com: http://amzn.to/1rvPuOs
Amazon.co.uk: http://amzn.to/1xtZoVH
Amazon.ca: http://amzn.to/1DRFLZm

Coming November...

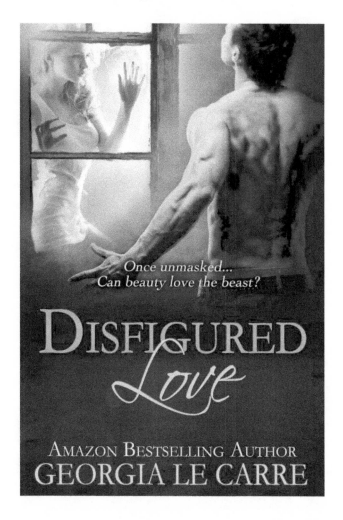

Once unmasked...
Can beauty love the beast?

DISFIGURED
Love

AMAZON BESTSELLING AUTHOR
GEORGIA LE CARRE

Synopsis

Disfigured Love

Once unmasked, can beauty love the beast?

My name is Lena Seagull. I should still be in school, hanging out with friends, meeting boys, falling in love—just like you. But on my eighteenth birthday my father sold me. Now, those are yesterday's dreams.

My home is a remote castle. And the man who owns me? I have never seen him.

Guy Hawk keeps his face hidden under a mask. At first, I knew only fear, but now his voice and touch make me unashamedly want him. Each night, his hired help blindfolds me, and takes me to his room. He whispers that I am beautiful and we have sex. It is wild and exciting, but when I awaken he is always gone.

He and his castle hold dark secrets that I must unravel, but what he fears most—being unmasked—is my deepest desire.

Will either of us survive the consequences of my desire?

Disfigured Love is a full-length standalone novel.

Disfigured Love

Georgia Le Carre

They must have the forbidden fruit, or paradise
will not be paradise for them.

—*Eugene Onegin*, Alexander Pushkin,

Once a upon a time...

there lived a...

Hawk

'Her eyes are a mutation. A beautiful mutation.'

It was in the early morning hours that Guy Hawk stopped working—he hardly slept anymore—and reached for the red envelope carefully laid at the edge of the desk. He placed it in front of him, and simply looked at it as if it held some great and frightening secret. In fact, its contents were prosaic and vulgar.

Some months ago, late one night, he had felt so unspeakably, unbearably lonely and unhappy that he had longed for the forgiving curves of a woman, any woman.

He had contacted the agency.

Ever since then bi-weekly a red envelope had arrived. But that intolerable loneliness of that fateful night had dissipated and he had looked at the photos inside it without interest, even with regret at his lapse in judgment, sometimes marvelling at the extent of his need. Never in his life had he paid for a woman and certainly not for an unwilling one. He had opened the envelopes and looked at those poor girls. And not once had he been even slightly tempted, though each one was exquisitely beautiful.

He sighed and tore it open. And began to tremble. The photographs fell from his nerveless hands and landed on his desk with a soft hiss.

The girl had cast her eyes out...and looked at him.

As if in a daze he picked up the photo and gazed at her silently, ravenously. At her enormous translucent gray eyes, the small, perfectly formed nose, the blonde hair, the large, plump lips, the flawlessly pale skin. How strange—he longed to know the smell of her skin, the taste of those full lips.

His hand—beautiful, large, strong, squarish, disbelieving—shook as his fingers traced the unsmiling outline of her face. He felt it then, as if the photo was alive, an impression of quiet grief. He lifted his fingers away, as if burnt, and frowned at the photo. She was effortlessly and utterly stunning. He must not fall under her spell. And yet it was already too late. The connection was instantaneous. Fate had waved its cruel, uncaring hand. He wanted her so bad it hurt. He reached for the other photo. She was wearing a bikini and high heels and standing with her arms to her sides in a bare room, the same one all the other girls had stood in. Leggy. Flawless. He turned the photo over.

Lena Seagull.

A strange smile crossed his face. How fitting. The hawk's prey is the seagull. Her age and vital statistics were displayed in English, French, Arabic and Chinese.

Age: 18
Height: 5'9", Dress Size: 6-8-10 Bust: 34 Waist: 24 Hips: 35.5
Shoes: 8, Hair: Blonde, Eyes: Dove Gray

He turned to his computer screen and tapped in his secret code. The encrypted message was only one word long: YES.

Almost instantly his phone rang.

'The auction will be held at 2.00 p.m. Friday. I believe there are two Arab princes who are also interested. She will not be cheap. What's your limit?'

'No limit.'

'Very good.'

Guy terminated the call and stared again at the girl.

He had never known such an irresistible desire before. He felt desperate to acquire her, brand her with body. And make her, his. His hand jerked with the sudden pain blooming in his chest. It ate like acid. It was so horrendous that tears filled his eyes and a howl escaped him. The sound vibrated and echoed around the cavernous room. The truth yawned like a black mouth: she would never come to love him. A beauty such as her was stardust, and could never love him. He was destined only for the part of the love struck fool at the hem of her skirt as she blazed past.

His good hand moved to stroke the raised scars on his face. He heard again the sickeningly angry screech of metal against metal, the explosion that had strangely brought with it a blissful silence and then the smell of his own flesh burning, burning, burning: watching his skin bubble, crackle, glow and smoke. He shuddered when he thought of the shimmering waves that rose from his flesh. He had sizzled and cooked like a piece of steak on a barbecue.

He hardened his heart.

He would have her, anyway. And think no more of it. She would be his pet. She would never come to know his heart. He laughed out loud. Unlike the sound of his anguish, which had throbbed with vital life, his laughter was empty and soulless. It disappeared into that deathly quiet castle and went to lie softly on his two secrets as they lay sleeping.

Lena Seagull

My name is not really Lena Seagull. Seagull is the nickname my father has been given by those who know him. While you are alive he will steal everything from you, and when you are dead he will steal even your eyeballs.

My first vivid memory is one of violence. When I was five years old I disobeyed my father. I refused to do something he wanted. I cannot remember what it was he wanted anymore. It was something small, insignificant. Definitely unimportant. He did not get angry. He nodded thoughtfully. Calmly he told my mother to put a pot of water on to boil. I remember her white face and her shaking hands clearly. She knew my father, you see. She put the water on to boil. He sat and smoked his pipe quietly.

'Is the water boiled yet?' he asked every so often.

'No,' she would say, her voice trembling with fear, and he would nod and carry on puffing on his pipe.

Eventually, she said, 'Yes. The water is ready.'

He put his pipe down carefully and stood. There was no anger. Perhaps he even sighed.

'Come here,' he called to my mother.

By now my mother's fear had communicated itself to me and I had begun to fidget, fret and hop from foot to foot in abject terror. I sobbed and cried out that I was sorry. I was very sorry. I would never again do such a thing. My father ignored me.

'Please, please,' I begged.

'Put the child on the chair,' he instructed.

My mother, with tears streaming down her cheeks, put me on the chair. Even then I think she already knew exactly what was about to happen because she smiled at me sadly, but with such love that I remember it to this day.

Reluctantly, she dragged her feet back to my father.

With the dizzying speed of a striking snake he grabbed her hand and plunged it into the boiling water. My mother's eyes bulged and she opened her mouth to scream, but the only sound that came out was the sound that someone makes when they are trying to vomit. While she writhed and twisted in agony he turned his beautiful blue eyes toward me. My father is an extremely handsome man.

The horror and shock silenced my screams and weighted me to my chair. For what seemed like eternity I could not move a single muscle. And then I began to shriek. A single piercing wail of terror. My father took my mother's hand and rushed her outside and plunged her hand into the snow. I ran out and watched them. My mother's face was ghostly white and her teeth were chattering uncontrollably. Then she turned to look at me and snapped them shut like a trap.

I was never the same after that day. I obeyed my father in all things...

For more news about Disfigured Love
& other releases sign up at the link below.
http://bit.ly/10e9WdE